AN IMPERFECT DEATH

J. J. FERNÁNDEZ

An Imperfect Death

To Michael

1

Monday, 9 January 2006
Time: 8.27 a.m.

THE END OF this story begins here, on any Monday in a cold January. There will always be a before and after in this fateful week, separated perhaps by an unexpected visit from the police.

A strong smell of sweat wakes me. I'm tangled up in the sheets and try to get my head out and breathe cleaner air. Last night, I forgot to draw the curtains, and the morning light is intense. I close my eyes again and reach my hand out to the other side of the bed, but it's cold. Tom has already stopped sleeping with me.

My tongue is swollen and dry, and a thousand drums beat at my temples. I try to find the glass of water that I usually leave on the bedside table before going to sleep. It falls on the floor and hits the parquet with a thud. Empty, like the bed. A trickle of sweat falls from my forehead. I get up and find myself still dressed in the black running tights and long-sleeved green nylon T-shirt I wore on my run yesterday.

I crawl into the bathroom, needles of pain pricking my body as I move. I open the drawer in the cabinet and rummage through cans, tubes and creams, then swallow a couple of aspirin, washing them down with cold water.

I lean forward and check the whiteboard with the distances I've run in the last four months. My chest swells. In less than a week I've increased the distance by almost a mile and gone over ten miles per run. I squeeze the marker hard. Will I make it to twenty-six miles for the marathon in Steyning in March? How many miles did I run yesterday? I write down another ten miles followed by a question mark.

Back in the bedroom, I put my brown leather travel bag on the bed. I take two shirts from the wardrobe, one charcoal grey and one cream. As I hold the hangers, a tickle goes up my fingers. Which shirt should I wear for the job interview? Undecided, I leave both shirts on the bed and look in the drawers for some underwear, a pair of T-shirts and some thick woollen socks. Then I pull out my light-blue jumper and blue jeans and lay them on the bed. They go well together and are comfortable for travelling. I take tonight's train ticket to Edinburgh from the drawer and my heart beats nervously. No one will notice my absence. Tom flew to Belfast on Sunday for a journalism conference and won't be back until next week. When he was talking on the phone to his colleague, unaware, I looked in his wallet for the plane ticket to check the day and time. This time he didn't lie.

I pull the chair out from the desk. Mum's coat is folded over it, an olive-green seventies-style wool-and-polyester coat. The shoulders, pockets and cuffs are decorated with red bands and matching buttons. After Mum's death, the coat became like a talisman for me. I examine it, and my eyes widen. The inner lining is torn on the right side and has a couple of dry mud stains the size of my hand. I take a deep breath. I'll take it to the dry cleaner's on my way to the nursing home to see Dad. Should I go to see Uncle Paddy too? Since he moved back from Malaysia, he's been a great support to me. Maybe I won't go – I don't want him to know about my trip for now.

I start the shower running and take off my clothes. Once the water is at the perfect temperature, the steam invites me in. I soap up my body and concentrate on the job interview. Am I ready for an interview after so many years? What if I'm offered the job? Am I up to being manager in one of the best hotels in Scotland? I'd have to move, but isn't that what I want? I can't continue to be an extension of Tom's life. I've had enough.

A dull thud startles me. Did it come from below or from the street? I turn off the water and tune my ear, but I only hear my breathing for a few seconds until another dull thud confirms that the noise is coming from downstairs. I drop the sponge and wrap myself in a towel, then ease the bathroom door open. I stick my head out and pull my wet hair back as if it'll increase my hearing. Out of nowhere footsteps come up the wooden stairs which creak with every step. My heart kicks and wants to run away. The sound intensifies and comes closer. I grab the knot of the towel tightly, with my fist on my chest, barely breathing. On impulse, I close the bathroom door, throw the lock and lean my back hard against the door. The footsteps get louder as they approach. My hands are trembling.

Someone knocks on the door and a baritone voice breaks the silence.

'Megan?' a familiar voice calls.

Tom's home? I open the door and catch my breath.

'Megan, did I scare you?'

I straighten and pull my towel a little higher and tighter.

'Don't you have to be in Belfast? What are you doing home?'

'My flight leaves this afternoon. I forgot to pick up some documents.' His voice trembles on the lie.

I don't move. Tom bends down and picks up the wet sponge. Natural light falls on his thick dark curls and reveals small strands of silver that I haven't noticed before. He gives the sponge back to me, and our fingers touch and mix with the moisture. My heart beats calmly again as my gaze fixes on Tom's fingers. The smell of oatmeal shampoo blends with his scent of wood, leather and lavender. I squeeze the sponge hard and a few drops randomly fall to the floor. I still haven't got used to his long absences because of his demanding job in that bloody newspaper.

His light-blue eyes search mine. 'Are you okay?'

I nod slowly. 'Don't you want to stay for breakfast?'

'I'm not hungry.' He looks at his watch. 'And I don't want to get stuck in traffic.'

'It's early. The traffic won't be so bad yet.'

'I don't want to be late.'

'For a flight leaving last night?'

He looks away. 'Megan, don't start with your paranoia. The flight leaves today, and I'm on schedule. I wanted to see how you were doing before I left.'

'If you want to be on time, you'd better leave.' I tighten the towel knot.

His eyes narrow as he takes in the clothes scattered on my bed alongside my travel bag. 'Are you going on a trip?'

I take a few seconds to respond. 'I'm organising the wardrobe.'

'And now you keep your clothes in your travel bag?'

'Weren't you in a hurry?'

Who is he to give me lessons in honesty? But he neither attacks me nor defends himself. His face shows only concern.

'You went for a run yesterday.' It sounds more like a statement than a question.

I look at the whiteboard with the ten miles on it and rest my gaze on the question mark. 'I guess so.' I cross my arms and keep my face serious.

'Well, I'm off.' He turns and lowers his head.

'Wait,' I say.

'Yes?' His tone becomes softer.

'No, nothing.' I exhale the words.

The truth is that I have nothing to say to him that I haven't already said. He comes over and kisses me on the forehead.

'Megan, it would be best if we talk when I get back.

Or when you get back.' And he disappears down the stairs with his head lowered.

The bang on the front door when it closes wakes me up from a dream.

———

After having some toast and a cup of tea for breakfast, I feel my headache is disappearing, but the aches and pains persist. I have to go to see Dad though. I go up to my room to get my bag and my mobile, but I can't find my watch.

On the Chinese sideboard in the entrance are my keys, on top of a small white envelope. I put the keys in my pocket and examine the envelope. There is no stamp or sender, only my name written on the back: *Megan*. It's not Tom's handwriting. The writing is more rounded and elongated. Inside the envelope is a cream-coloured card signed by my neighbour.

> *What a shock!*
> *I hope you're feeling better.*
> *I'll come by later.*
> *Margie*

I blink several times. How inappropriate and curious Margie is. Retired and with too much free time on her hands. Doesn't she have better things to do now than write meaningless notes? Not wanting to miss the bus, I automatically put the note in my pocket, tuck in my scarf, put on my hat and coat and grab my bag and my mum's coat. When I put my hand on the doorknob, the doorbell announces that there's someone behind it waiting for me to open it. I take my hand off the doorknob and count to ten, but the doorbell rings again, insistently now. I give up and open the door.

In front of me are two policemen.

Here begins the most tragic week of my life.

2

Monday, 9 January 2006
Time: 9.58 a.m.

'GOOD MORNING. MRS EVANS?' says the older policeman. He's short, with a square jaw and abundant grey,
almost white, hair. His partner – much younger, with
chubby cheeks and the appearance of a university
student – stands behind him.

'What can I do for you?' I ask with a false polite
tone.

I don't have time for this. I have so many things to
do: go to the dry cleaner's, see Dad, prepare for the
interview, stop by Sophie's Oxfam charity shop to say
goodbye.

'I'm Sergeant Warren Jones, and this is Constable
Andy Reed,' says the older man. They're holding up
their IDs, with photos, names and numbers that I can't
decipher. 'We'd like to talk to you.'

Talk to me about what? I take a step back and my lips open, but no words come out of my mouth.

'It's important,' he insists. His voice not only conveys authority but also concern. The bag with the coat slips slowly from my fingers and falls to the ground. I bend down and pick it up while my brain tries to interpret the meaning of 'important'.

'Please come in.'

Sergeant Jones enters, keeping his chest out. The younger policeman, with his long legs, follows, imitating the short steps of his superior.

'Please sit down.' I have a quick look around the living room. Everything seems to be in order. I leave my hat on the oak table and run my hand through my hair. It's still wet.

'Would you like something to drink? Tea?' It immediately feels like a silly question.

'Thank you—'

'No thanks, Mrs Evans.' Sergeant Jones' voice, dry and professional, cuts off his subordinate's words.

'What did we agree on?' My eyes jump from one policeman to the other and their mere presence makes me uncomfortable.

'No thanks,' repeats Sergeant Jones, stretching his lips in a forced attempt to simulate a poorly rehearsed smile. 'Are you alone?'

'Yes.'

'Where did you say your husband was?'

His question puts me on guard. Half an hour ago I was arguing with Tom, and now the police are asking about him. I hope he didn't get into any trouble with them because of his work at the newspaper.

'I don't remember mentioning my husband. Has something happened to Tom?'

'We are not here to talk about your husband.'

'Who then?'

'Your uncle,' the youngest policeman interrupts.

'My uncle? Why do you want to talk about my uncle?'

I'm paralysed. Sergeant Jones fires a disapproving look at his subordinate. Then his green eyes meet mine and I have time to see something softer in his gaze before they move away and land on the notepad that he takes out of his pocket. The muscles in his face tighten and he says, 'Mrs Megan Evans, we do not have good news.'

The metallic sound of a mobile phone cuts through the room. Constable Reed looks at the screen and holds it up to his superior, who signals for him to go out and answer it.

'Give us a moment, please,' says Sergeant Jones, raising his forefinger.

I nod. Constable Reed leaves the door ajar and the sound of a leaf blower mixes with a winter chill. I put my hands in my pockets and tense my heel, which hits the floor like a speeding clock. Sergeant Jones watches me for a few seconds that feel like hours.

When Constable Reed comes back in, the colour of his cheeks is more intense and my heart shrinks. What happened to Uncle Paddy? He sits next to his boss and his lips form the almost inaudible word, 'Positive.' Sergeant Jones nods and without looking up from his notebook, continues with the same tone of authority.

'We will not keep you waiting any longer. We have to inform you that this morning a neighbour in the area found Patrick Brady in a car.'

'What car?'

'His car.'

'Has Uncle Paddy been in a car accident?'

'Not exactly. Let me finish, please.' He presses the notepad and continues, 'We are currently investigating, to identify the cause.'

'The cause of what? I don't understand.'

Constable Reed lowers his gaze even further and Sergeant Jones continues, 'The coroner will be ruling on the cause of your uncle's death. I'm very sorry.'

The information enters my brain very slowly and the words echo in my mind: *Important. Uncle. Positive. Neighbour. Car. Coroner.* My heel tapping is getting more intense.

'His death?' I repeat aloud, as if trying to assimilate the meaning of the word 'death'.

'We are very sorry. Would you like to contact your husband?'

'No.' The door is still open, and a cold breeze blows in and sends a chill down my back.

'Well, maybe another relative?'

'Did you say "death"?' I repeat, louder. 'It must be a mistake.'

'Unfortunately not.'

At that very moment my brain clicks, a click that

brings the words together and gives meaning to the phrases, and just milliseconds later, my heart thuds.

'If it wasn't a traffic accident, what was he doing in his car?'

'I can't answer that, but what I can assure you is that we have received confirmation of his death.'

Constable Reed puts a hand on my shoulder and says, 'Please sit down. We'd better have that tea. Where…?'

I drop myself into the navy-blue velvet chair and point to the kitchen. 'Up in the cabinet on the right.'

Sergeant Jones stands up, but before he can make an excuse, Constable Reed steps forward.

'Boss, it'll just be five minutes.'

Sergeant Jones doesn't answer. He sits down again, closes his notebook and takes a deep breath as if preparing to start a bad day.

A few minutes later, the kettle sings, then the cups hit the glass coffee table and wake me up from a bad dream.

'The tea is ready,' Constable Reed says.

I take the cup and the heat burns my fingertips slightly. I blow and take a sip. Good tea has to be bitter, Uncle Paddy used to say.

'How old was your uncle?' Sergeant Jones asks. I don't reply so he continues his interrogation. 'Was he an older man? A Catholic priest?'

'Sixty-four years old, and not a priest. He was a sacristan, but he retired. He spent some periods in Steyning, when he wasn't working.'

'But you said he was retired?'

'Yes, he's been out of the sacristy for years.'

Constable Reed raises a shy smile that makes his cheeks even rounder and more jovial. 'Forgive my ignorance. What is a sacristan?'

'He was in charge of assisting the priest in the care and cleaning of the church, the sacristy, and also of preparing the celebration of the Catholic Mass. After my mother passed away a few years ago, he decided to change the course of his life and join a group of Catholic missionaries based in Malaysia, who helped with the schooling of girls. He spent long periods of time in the slums of Kuala Lumpur.' I put the cup on a coaster on the coffee table. 'Who was the neighbour who found him?'

Sergeant Jones speaks up. 'As I told you, a neighbour in the area found your uncle early this morning. The car was badly parked at the side of a local road that crosses the Findon Valley. The neighbour thought it was strange, so he approached the car and found your uncle's body.'

'Just like that? I still don't understand it. Are you sure it's my uncle?'

Sergeant Jones' jaw exerts such pressure on his thin lips that they disappear. With his right hand he slowly pushes the teacup towards me and says in a forced tone, 'Thank you for the tea. You are very kind. We have to go.'

I get up quietly and take the cups into the kitchen. The dishwasher is full, so I leave them in the sink. The other day I saw one of those American documentaries about medical errors. It was about patients who were diagnosed with a fatal disease by mistake.

In the background, Sergeant Jones' dry cough pulls me out of my thoughts, and I return to the living room.

'Following protocol, we are required to inform you that we need a family member to identify the body and sign the death certificate.' He breathes deeply. 'Perhaps if you contact your husband or a family member you could—'

'My husband is on a trip. I'll do it.'

'You should at least inform your husband.'

After the discussion this morning, the last thing I want at this point is for Tom to get involved in my personal affairs.

'I said I'll do it.' I fetch the hat I left on the oak table no more than twenty minutes ago and put it on.

'Then, if you would be so kind, please come with us,' Sergeant Jones says.

3

Monday, 9 January 2006
Time: 10.27 a.m.

A LATE BUT persistent mist covers the street. The blue, white and flashing yellow of the police car shines in front of my house. The cold flutters in my face like restless butterflies, and my legs, clumsy and reluctant, manoeuvre me into the back seat. The black plastic upholstery sticks to my trousers like a spider's web trapping its prey.

'We'll be there in twenty minutes,' Constable Reed says in an encouraging voice.

And then what?

As we're about to leave, a shadow hammers insistently on the other side of the glass and my lungs fill up with a sudden burst of air that tastes like stale coffee and vomit. It's my neighbour Margie. Her breath on the window blurs the expression on her face into a mixture of surprise and curiosity.

'Not now,' I manage to mutter, and Margie watches as I'm driven away in the police car.

I feel her card in my pocket and remember the words:

> *What a shock!*
> *I hope you're feeling better.*
> *I'll come by later.*
> *Margie*

What 'shock' is she talking about? Her note doesn't make sense. Nothing that's happening makes sense. I miss my mum, but Mum isn't here. And Dad is here, but it's as if he weren't. Tom is around, but I don't want him to be. And now they tell me that Uncle Paddy isn't here any more. Sometimes I feel like I'm not here either. I put my hand on my heart and repeat to myself, 'Where are you, Uncle Paddy?'

My uncle helped my mother, his little sister, when Dad was away. He took care of me and my sister Katherine and instilled us with values and respect for our peers. He gave support to the community, especially the younger ones. He travelled to Malaysia many times and worked in schools in the poorest slums in the country. He wasn't perfect – he had a bad temper, like many Irishmen – but he was a good man and believed in the goodness of people. Now he is no longer.

I breathe so deep that my chest hurts.

Sometimes I feel like I'm not either. Sometimes I feel like I want to run, and many other times I want to escape.

Nothing makes sense.

Cautiously, I try to open the window a couple of millimetres and throw Margie's stupid note away without being seen by the police, but the handle doesn't budge.

'It's not broken,' says Constable Reed through the Perspex partition. 'It's for safety reasons.'

I close my hand and hide the note. Sergeant Jones drives quietly, watching me in the rear-view mirror. What is he thinking about? Did he see me trying to throw the note out the window?

'You should contact your husband,' he repeats with the same authoritarian tone.

I don't reply. Through the car window, I see the clouds swell with water and darken the sky. I press my lips together and swallow hard. I'm not going to talk to Tom. I have another, less humiliating option. I take my phone out of my bag and call my sister Katherine. A lump loaded with pride makes its way down my throat. Six rings later, the call goes to voicemail. I hang up. I hate leaving voice messages. The last time I spoke to Katherine was over six months ago, when I was hospitalised, and our relationship has grown even colder since then.

I call a second and third time, but she still doesn't pick up.

At the fourth attempt, I give in.

'Katherine, it's Megan. Call me when you get this message. Call me, okay? It's important.'

Sergeant Jones keeps watching me in the rear-view mirror.

'These things don't happen here,' he says as he manoeuvres the car into a parking space.

'What things?'

'I've been on the force for almost forty years, Mrs Evans. And in four months, I will retire. I've seen it all.'

His tired green eyes jump from the rear-view mirror to Constable Reed.

'What doesn't happen here?' I persist.

He gets out of the car and opens my door, then offers his hand to help me out. 'The dead die at home, or in a nursing home or in a hospital. They do not die in a car.' He breathes deep and long. 'Your uncle was probably not well enough to be driving.'

What was Uncle Paddy doing in his car last night?

I put my hand on the seat and get out on my own.

4

Monday, 9 January 2006
Time: 10.58 a.m.

'CONSTABLE REED,' Sergeant Jones says, 'can you please leave us alone?'

The young constable quietly disappears behind a door that seems to squeak for help.

'Please sit down,' Sergeant Jones tells me.

I perch on the edge of a chair at an old office table. Next to Sergeant Jones sits a small man with the face of a university professor. He's holding a worn brown leather briefcase and is looking at me through thick, heavy glasses.

Sergeant Jones continues talking. 'This is Dr Brown from Brighton Regional Hospital. We don't have a coroner in this area, and he has kindly come at short notice.'

'Good morning,' Dr Brown says, with a certain

cautious tone. 'First of all, I would like to offer you my condolences. How are you?'

I put my bag in my lap and squeeze it over my knees. My aches and pains persist, the harsh taste of the news of my uncle's death persists, and the thought of talking to my sister sets my teeth on edge.

'How do I feel?' I lick my dry lips and shake my head. 'I haven't thought about it yet.'

'I understand. Mrs Evans, I will not keep you waiting any longer.' Dr Brown opens his briefcase, puts some papers on the table and runs his fingers over the report as if reading Braille. 'As you have been informed, your Uncle Patrick was found dead this morning in his car.'

My hands are damp with sweat and I'm losing the grip on my bag which is like heavy marble.

Sergeant Jones interrupts. 'During the investigation, no external agent was found.'

'That's right,' confirms Dr Brown. 'I personally went to examine the body and confirmed the police report.' He puts his hands together, lacing his fingers, and stares at me. 'Your uncle died of natural causes.'

My eyes narrow as if trying to focus on a new situation. 'Did you say natural causes?'

'Correct,' Sergeant Jones says. 'That speeds up the process.'

'What natural causes?' I ask Dr Brown.

'The cause of your Uncle Patrick's death is cardiac arrest caused by prolonged apnoea.'

He pauses as if waiting for me to nod and confirm that I understand his words. I say nothing. I try to swallow, but my throat is dry. My face is carved in the same stone I hold on my lap. Only the sweat from my hands and the intense stiffness of my legs make me lucid.

Sergeant Jones looks down at his watch and Dr Brown continues, 'Well, it's apnoea, or respiratory arrest. In this case, as it is a prolonged apnoea, it affects other vital functions such as the heart.'

No one says anything. The tapping of Sergeant Jones' fingers on the desk is mixed with the smell of wet carpet.

'Just like that?' I ask in disbelief.

'Do you know if your uncle suffered from asthma?' Dr Brown asks.

'My uncle only suffered from the misery of others. I didn't even know he had asthma, let alone serious enough to cost him his life.'

They look at each other.

'I have to admit that these are rare cases.' The doctor puts his glasses on and goes through the report again. 'In the medical report, there is no evidence that your Uncle Patrick suffered from chronic asthma, so there is greater certainty that this is a rare case.'

The taste of bile rises in my mouth.

'Certainty? A rare case? Are you assuming that my uncle left the house and had an asthma attack?'

'It's winter. The temperatures have dropped, and excessive cold can affect the lungs.'

'And the cold killed my uncle?'

The doctor takes off his glasses. 'Not the cold directly, Mrs Evans, but an unexpected asthma attack.'

'And within this certainty you have, do you have another theory?' I cross my arms.

Dr Brown gives himself a few seconds before replying. 'We don't do theories. The report is based on facts.' He points at it with his glasses. 'I just collect evidence and write up the autopsy. It's not the first case and unfortunately it won't be the last.'

I'm gasping for air. Is there anyone who can open a damn window? Sergeant Jones' voice prevails in the conversation.

'Mrs Evans, the car is in perfect condition. There are no signs of accident or a criminal act.' He pauses and takes a deep breath. 'Your uncle felt bad, stopped the car in the gutter and minutes later died of an asthma attack. I can tell you louder, but not clearer.'

I look up at him as quickly as a dagger hits the target. 'My uncle never drives after dark.'

'Mrs Evans, let's calm down.' Dr Brown raises his palms. 'I understand the difficulty of accepting the loss of a loved one. I have seen many strange cases in my career. Apnoea is not uncommon. His prolonged apnoea was due to a severe asthma attack, causing the airways to close and preventing the lungs from performing their function of exchanging oxygen and carbon dioxide. This affected other vital organs such as the heart, resulting in cardiorespiratory arrest and inevitably death. I am truly sorry.'

I shake my head without saying a word.

'Do you still want to see your uncle?' he asks as he looks at me.

They tell me my uncle is dead. He is dead, I repeat

to myself. Dead, I repeat again and again. Could they be wrong? Is there any chance, however small, that they could have the wrong person?

I hide the pain of my stiffness and stand up with determination. 'I've already told Sergeant Jones that I do.'

5

Monday, 9 January 2006
Time: 5.22 p.m.

FROM THE NAVY-BLUE VELVET ARMCHAIR, I feel absolute
silence stretching out in the house. It's a different silence,
not the kind I like to hear when I'm alone. This silence
tastes different. I take the last sip of tea. It's already cold.
Its taste is the same as this silence that stifles the living
room and makes me smaller. A bitter taste.

The morgue and my house are closer than I
thought. There, I found my uncle lying on a metal bed,
but I didn't dare touch him. His face was white wax
bathed in a grimace of terror. Terror of his death.

Sergeant Jones' hands rested on my shoulders and
steered me to a corner with a folding table. He handed
me a pen, I signed, and he put me in a cab back home.

Now I reread the official note with my uncle's name
on it and the cause of his death: cardiac arrest caused by
prolonged apnoea.

Why did he take his car out at night?

I call Katherine from my home phone. 'Katherine, it's me. Can you please call me? It's urgent. We need to talk about Uncle Paddy.'

The light from the answering machine blinks, and I play the messages.

"Megan, it's me," Tom's voice says. "I'm at the airport. The plane is delayed, so I'm taking it easy. I'm sorry about this morning."

I notice that the couch blanket is wrinkled and out of place next to the wicker basket. Maybe Tom fell asleep on the couch and missed his plane. Why lie?

"Megan, we have to talk at some point and—"

Message deleted.

Someone is knocking at the door. I turn off the lamp and stand still. They knock again, insistently, instead of using the bell. I look through the peephole and it's Margie, my neighbour. She knocks again.

'Margie, it's not a good time,' I say through the door.

'I know it's late, but I wanted to stop by.'

'Really, we'd be better talking tomorrow.'

'I won't leave until you tell me how you are.'

I shrug my shoulders in defeat, take a deep breath, then open the door. Margie enters the house with short but determined steps. She has curlers in her white hair, covered with a plastic wrap. Her look is serious and inquisitive.

'Come in.'

'How are you, dear?'

'I am. I guess.'

'Well, let's have some tea and you can tell me all about it.'

A grimace escapes me. Cups of tea don't bring me good news. 'What about Alfred?' I ask.

'Watching TV.' Her gaze flutters around the dining room. 'That man will be the death of me. He doesn't want to take his pills, but the doctor has already told him it's the only way to control his cholesterol.' She sighs. 'Well, not only that. He should also stop stuffing his face with cheese.' She sits down at the dining table and continues as I make tea. 'This sciatica is going to take me to the grave. Men, my dear, the older they get, the harder they are to handle.' She looks around the room again.

'Tom isn't home,' she states more than asks.

'No. He's on a trip.'

'Well.' She wrinkles her forehead.

'Here's your tea.'

The day Tom and I moved into this house ten years ago, Margie brought us a carrot cake, some homemade pastries and a dozen indiscreet questions. The tradition has continued on each of our birthdays. Including the indiscreet questions.

'You took the teabag out too soon.'

'Oh, I'm sorry,' I reply in a flat voice.

'Never mind.' She leaves the cup on the table and puts her hands together. 'I'm worried. Very worried.'

'About Alfred?'

'I didn't come here to talk about Alfred,' she says, shaking her head. 'I've come to talk about you. You gave us quite a shock yesterday, and today I saw you in a police car. Tom isn't here. And as I said, I'm worried.' She pauses and her tone becomes sweeter. 'What's going on, dear?'

I put her note on the table. My fingers swell with blood as if a colony of a thousand ants were running through the veins of my hand, and a wave of heat pushes my words out.

'Uncle Paddy has died.'

'Oh, my goodness. How so? Poor man. I didn't know he was so bad.' She puts her hand on mine and leans forward as if she wants to hear the news more closely.

'I didn't know either,' I answer.

'Forgive me for intruding—'

'He was short of breath and his heart stopped,' I answer before she asks.

'Suddenly?'

'That's how it seems.'

'And the police car?'

'The police came to give me the news this morning.'

'Oh.' Her hand squeezes mine. 'What does Tom say about all this?'

I slip my hand out of hers, and she feels the note she wrote me this morning.

'Well, he's on a trip.'

'Yes, you told me. But when will he be back?'

'Soon,' I lie. 'Very soon.'

She takes a napkin from the table and waves it for me to dry my forehead. 'What bad timing. Have you seen the gynaecologist?'

The sweat on my brow doesn't lie. 'I've got aches

and pains and I've taken a hot bath to relax my muscles.'

'Nonsense. A bath won't fix it. It's the menopause, my dear. Don't be fooled. What's going on with all the running now? Excess is not good, not good. That's how you were yesterday when Tom picked you up. You had collapsed. We were all scared.' She raises her note like a soccer referee raises a red card.

My mouth opens and my eyes narrow. 'Tom picked me up yesterday? Where from?

'Out there.' She points to the main door. 'I told Alfred to come out with me to see what was going on. Don't you remember? It looked like the devil was chasing you. You were pounding on the door shouting "Tom, Tom, Tom".' A crude imitation of my voice comes out of her mouth.

Tom didn't say anything to me about that this morning. I remember now. The damn hot flush knocked me out and I was alarmed. It had never happened to me before while I was running. My blood felt like whips beating my soul into a stone oven. Maybe I got scared, full of rage, and took it out on Tom. I just wanted to lie down, curl up in myself and disappear into oblivion. Sleeping helps you to forget.

'It's not the first time that's happened to me. It started a month ago.'

'And it won't be the last time either, my dear. My mother, may she rest in peace, had a tough menopause too. Then she had complications with ovarian cancer and, well…' She sees my confusion and continues, 'But, oh dear, that's another story. What are you going to do?'

'Keep running, if I can.'

'I know that. You are very stubborn. I mean about your uncle.'

'The Mass is on Sunday. I still need to meet Father Jonathan. He'll be in charge of the arrangements.'

Margie gets out of the chair with difficulty. 'Well, you've been standing for a while now, so I'll go.' Then she notices my travel bag under the sideboard, next to the door. 'Tom went on a trip and forgot his suitcase.'

I feel heat flush my face and remain mute, waiting for the earth to swallow me up. Margie takes small steps to the door as if taking time to find the right words. She turns, and her expression is a bittersweet, motherly mix of half disappointment, half understanding.

'If you're going to be around and you need something, I'm here.' Her voice becomes an unexpected whisper. 'Dear, listen to me well. I just want you to be okay, you know, just like before. Tom is a lovely man and you've always been a very good match. Wouldn't your uncle want that for you? There's always a reason for things.' A shadow crosses her face. 'Remember that Oliver doesn't have Amy any more.'

My chest tightens when I hear Amy's name.

Then Margie closes the door and I'm left alone.

I run my fingers over the surface of the suitcase. It's a vintage case made of hard brown cardboard, with a metal rivet in each corner. It belonged to Mum, and came with her from Ireland to England almost forty years ago. I find it hard to get rid of Mum's things. Besides, it's still in perfect condition. It will bring me luck. I leave tonight and will be back on Wednesday, just enough time to empty Uncle Paddy's house, do the paperwork and attend the funeral on Sunday. I touch the leather handle and Margie's words repeat in my head. 'There is always a reason for things.' Is this what I want? I hold the handle tightly. In a few hours the cab will pick me up to go to the station. I just have to wait. Wait for the cab, wait for a change. I have to be brave.

6

Monday, 9 January 2006
Time: 6.45 p.m.

Katherine still doesn't answer. Her mobile is off. Either she hasn't received my messages, or if she has received them, she doesn't want to answer, and that's not a good sign.

The floor in the hall is cold. I've turned the heating off because I'll be away for a few days. I stretch my legs out on the parquet, put my arms together and rest my cheek on the suitcase. It seems that the mothballs Mum used as a young mother are still active. This suitcase has more life than me.

In an hour and a half, the cab will arrive to take me to the station, to catch the train from Brighton to Edinburgh via London. Nine hours of travel on a night train, northward from the south of the country. There's something magical about night trains. They travel in the darkness through fields, valleys and towns as though in a dreamlike journey from one land to another through a long black tunnel, and when you wake up, you're there. You've been transported to another time and place. Like in a story with a happy ending.

My happy ending?

In my legs I have ants doing a military march, and in my stomach an army of butterflies are at war.

I get up, put on some chill-out music and pour myself a glass of wine. The wine will relax me. I kill time reading the news on my laptop. Another gathering has been arranged in solidarity with the victims of the 7/7 attack in London. That morning, newspapers had announced that the next Olympic Games would be held in London in 2012. It was much-anticipated good news that a few hours later was stained with blood. I raise my glass. In the dim light, the wine has an intense dark red colour. It runs through my veins like an anaesthetic, calming the memories.

That morning, ambulances picked up more than a hundred dead and hundreds of wounded that were scattered in the streets in London. They couldn't keep up. Ambulances came from other parts of the country and wandered around lost, their lights and sirens mixing as they looked for the nearest hospital.

Has Oliver gone to the gathering in memory of Amy? I don't think so. He's been locked in his house, locked up in his misery. I take another sip of the blood-coloured wine and continue reading the newspaper article. Amy's photo appears in the panel of victims. She seems to be still alive, with her almost albino blonde hair, pale blue cat eyes and skin as white as silk paper.

She looks like an angel. I press my lips together. Unfortunately, she only looked that way. As I finish the glass, the wine tastes like metal to me.

An hour until the cab arrives.

I go to Wikipedia. What is asthma? There are different types of asthma, depending on the frequency. Unstable, occupational, allergic asthma. There was no record of Uncle Paddy suffering from chronic asthma, and to my knowledge, he was never allergic to anything. I continue reading and find 'seasonal asthma'. Dr Brown confirmed that Uncle Paddy suffered from seasonal asthma caused by low temperatures.

Through the windows of the kitchen, the cold is dark blue, almost black, bathed in the pale light of small lamp posts. The same cold that killed my uncle. I shake my head. It all seems unreal.

A shadow wanders down the lonely street. It stops, continues and stops again as if it were lost. I blink and adjust my eyes to the darkness of the street. The shadow has the silhouette of a large man with a clumsy walk. I sneak over to the dining room window and see my reflection in the glass. I turn off the light but there's nothing beyond it. The silhouette has disappeared.

There's half a bottle of wine left. The hands of the wall clock seem to move like they're alive and I feel a bit dizzy.

When I leave the glass in the sink, the automatic light in the doorway turns on, but there is no one in the street, and my body contracts and stops in a reflex action. I wait for someone to knock on the door. I wait to hear a sound. A noise. Something that explains the sudden light.

I look through the peephole but there is no one at the entrance. Only silence.

It could be a fox or a cat. We've been having problems with foxes for months. They sneak out at night and look in the rubbish. They break the bags and leave the gardens full of rubbish. Our containers were replaced last month, and the new ones are taller and heavier, so I thought we wouldn't have that problem any longer.

Curiosity pushes me to open the door and the intense light from the spotlight by the entrance dazzles me. There is no fox or cat. Just a wall of icy air and a feeling of unease. An unexpected shiver hits my body and I clench my jaw. At the end of the street the silhouette of a big man disappears as he turns the corner. I relax the muscles of my face, but a drop of sweat runs down my forehead. My heartbeat hits my temples, and heat invades my body. Another hot flush. I resign myself to it and start to close the door, but something flashes on the step, reflecting the light. I bend over and my legs cramp. I get down on my knees and touch the shiny object. It's my watch! The quartz watch that Tom gave me on our fifth anniversary. I hold it as if my fingers were two lab tweezers, and when I look closely, my heart wrinkles like the face of a girl with a broken doll and my joy is replaced with guilt. The watch is broken. The face is missing, and the hands are stopped. I grab on to the door frame and stand up.

I turn my head to look up and down the street. I'm cloaked by the dark blue of the night, splashed by the weak lights of the surrounding houses. How did my watch get here? Did the mysterious man bring it? Does he know me? This is absurd. If he knows who I am and where I live, he could have knocked on the door. I caress the watch, but what value does a broken watch have?

The time reads 6.47 p.m. on 8 January. Last night. That's the time I got home after my run. I was exhausted. The light in the doorway goes out, but another light comes on inside me with a more logical explanation: when I knocked on the door, I hit the watch, and it fell and broke.

I feel the ground in the entrance looking for the watch face. The light comes back on, but there's no trace of it. I keep trying, sweeping the entranceway with my fingertips, but only feel the rough, dusty ground. The cold outside mixes with my internal hot flush and I sweat in anxiety. I'll have it fixed – I'll replace the hands and put a new face on it.

A jumble of nerves presses my stomach, and they want to escape. I clench the watch tightly in my fist. Fear mixes with sweat and my instinct defeats my logic.

My instinct whispers in my ear that the watch didn't fall off on my doorstep. It whispers to me that someone brought it here. Someone who knows me. Someone who doesn't want me to know who he is. Someone who maybe knew Uncle Paddy too.

I secure both locks on the door, close the windows then take the bottle of wine and go up to my room. I turn the key in that door too and turn off the light. The doorbell rings. My cab has arrived.

A desire, or perhaps a curiosity stronger than fear,

grabs me and doesn't let me leave Findon. Who brought me the watch? Why did my dead uncle show up in his car? Are these too many coincidences or am I going crazy?

I take a good swallow from the bottle of wine. I feel a pleasant looseness in my legs. The bell rings again. I ignore it. Minutes later the cab disappears.

The wine gives me the strength to call Tom, but I hang up right away. What do I do? I think again, and decide to call him. It goes straight to voicemail. He'll be flying to Ireland. I don't leave a message.

I swallow and make another call, this time to Edinburgh.

'This is Megan Evans. I have an interview for the position of manager tomorrow morning and unfortunately, it's going to be impossible for me to attend… If I wait… Yes, of course I am still interested, very interested, but an unexpected family matter has come up. My uncle has passed away. Would it be possible to postpone the interview until next week…? I understand … of course… Thank you. Tuesday morning then.'

I take the rest of the bottle in one gulp. Then I put my mobile phone on the table, lie down and close my eyes. I press the watch to my chest.

'There's always a reason for things.'

It's raining hard outside. Everything is spinning, and with it, I fall asleep and disappear.

7

Tuesday, 10 January 2006
Time: 9.47 a.m.

KATHERINE HAS DISAPPEARED. She hasn't answered my calls or messages. She's been swallowed up by work, or the earth. I'm fidgeting with an old card from her company at Canary Wharf that I found in a drawer in Tom's desk. The card smells like Coco Chanel, too heavy and dominant. Katherine still doesn't know that Uncle Paddy died in his car. She would never believe the story of a burly, clumsy man bringing my broken watch to the front door and then disappearing. She's too pragmatic to see beyond her own situation.

My sister Katherine's life shifts between investment projects in the Third World, meetings in London's financial centre and business trips to exotic places, and when she's not doing that, she's attending art galleries and sipping champagne. This is how Katherine paints her own life. She has lived in Dublin, Belfast, San Francisco,

New York and Singapore. In that order, if I remember correctly. She's never lived in the same place for more than five years. She's been in London for almost five, which is a miracle.

She cannot refuse to come to her uncle's funeral. I pick up the cordless phone at home and dial the number.

'Good morning. Could I please speak to Katherine Hudson?'

'One moment, please.' The receptionist puts me on hold and I hear Louis Armstrong's 'What a Wonderful World'.

I stop walking around like a military man and sit on the couch. For a couple of minutes, Armstrong's voice hums in my ears, and my eyes land on the enigmatic painting Katherine painted for me when I turned thirty and moved in with Tom. It covers the wall above the light brown leather sofa. The painting depicts a row of five newborn girls, each inside a sock hanging on a washing line in the countryside. Their eyes are closed and their faces are carved in pink porcelain. They sleep peacefully like little cherubs inside their socks of different colours: blue, orange, yellow, red and green. They look like freshly washed clothes hung out to dry. Katherine said she was inspired by our childhood, although personally I don't remember putting babies in a washing machine and then hanging them up on the line.

Katherine is not only an artist, she is also a closed book.

'What department?' the receptionist asks in a hurry.

'I don't know.'

'If you don't know, I can't help you.'

'It's an emergency,' I insist.

The receptionist huffs and her voice quickens. 'Madam, this is Canary Wharf. All calls are an emergency.'

'She's one of the heads of the investment department. Please, it's a family matter.'

'Why don't you call her directly on her mobile phone?'

The harder I hold the phone, the more I try to make my voice sound like a plea.

'I don't know how many times I've called her on her mobile. I'm her sister and I need to talk to her. Please try to understand that this is an emergency.'

A long pause on the other end of the line takes me back to my childhood. Katherine was always a free bird, difficult to catch. When she was fourteen years old, Mum and Dad sent her to a boarding school in Ireland. It seemed strange to me that she didn't refuse. In Ireland, she continued her studies in economics and found her first job. The years and distance separated us. As an adult, when I tried to reconnect with her again after Mum's sudden death, I lost her.

'I'll put you through to the investment department. Please wait a moment.'

'Thank you very much.'

My voice is as tense as it was the last time Katherine and I dined together, in a restaurant in the West End in London. Her mobile rang every five minutes as I was trying to find the right moment to tell her that I was pregnant. I asked her to turn it off and she questioned whether my life was more important than hers. Her gaze was as bright as Dad's eyes when he was young. I suppose I didn't have to be so abrupt with her. She didn't find out about my pregnancy until a week later, when I was hospitalised.

'Good morning, financial products department.'

'Can I speak to Katherine Hudson?'

'Do you have a telephone appointment?'

'It's a family matter. It'll only take a second.'

'One moment.'

My mobile rings and my heart swells and stops. It has to be Katherine. I run to the kitchen counter, but as soon as I grab the phone, I push it away. It's not her. My shoulders drop and my face wrinkles. It's Tom. I ignore him.

The music cuts out and I hear a voice at the other end of the phone.

'She's busy. Shall I pass her a message?'

'No, tell her it's her sister Megan. I need to speak to her urgently,' I insist.

'I didn't know Katherine had a sister. One moment, please. I'll try again.'

Her voice is more pleasant.

I pinch my lips while I wait. This time there's no music, only a silence as uncomfortable as the waiting room of a hospital. Katherine didn't visit me when I was hospitalised. She was on a trip. She did call me twice. The first time I talked to her for five minutes between aeroplanes. The second time Tom picked it up, and she didn't call again.

'I'm very sorry, but she just went into her morning meeting and gave me direct instructions not to pass on any calls.'

'Not even from her sister?' I ask, half frustrated, half surprised.

'All I can say is that I am very sorry. Whatever message you give me, I will pass it directly to her when the meeting is over. But I don't know when it will end.' A short pause. 'I assume you have her mobile phone number?'

A flow of bile is crawling up my throat. I swallow and my chin rises in front of the picture of freshly washed babies hanging from a washing line. There is something twisted among all that beauty.

I clench the phone like I clench my teeth, and respond.

'Tell her Uncle Paddy died.'

———

I put on tights, a polyester shirt, a cap, Lycra gloves, a bumbag, my neck warmer and a windproof jacket. On top of the kitchen table is the quartz watch, along with my mobile phone. Tom has sent a text message.

"You called last night. I hope you're okay. Kisses."

I take a green apple and bite into it, making small circles with my fingertip on the watch. The missing face is like something missing in our relationship. Can it be fixed? I reread Tom's message, then put the watch in my jacket pocket and write back, 'I'm fine. Kisses.'

I put on my trainers, press the watch hard and look

through the peephole before opening the door. I bite my lower lip.

Imagination is the worst enemy of fear.

Why did Uncle Paddy take his car out after dark?

I open the door and run to my uncle's house.

8

Tuesday, 10 January 2006
Time: 11.21 a.m.

MY LUNGS ARE ALMOST polar cold. According to the police report, the same cold that caused Uncle Paddy's death. I lift my neck warmer to protect my neck, nose and mouth. What made him leave the house at night?

The pavement is slippery from the overnight rain, and I step with care. A few metres down, I pass by Oliver and Amy's house. It looks like Oliver is not at work as his Mercedes is parked outside. The house is in a contemporary style, designed by Oliver's brother and paid for by Amy's father. A blush heats my cheeks. In the past, Tom would sometimes invite Oliver and Amy over for dinner. It was a different time and we lived among lies.

I keep a steady pace and cross Findon's main street, a long road lined on each side with a string of trees spaced with symmetrical precision, and then I run into the valley. My heartbeat has stabilised, and I increase my pace. The blood hits my temples like a ticking clock. I'm no longer cold. I leave the valley behind, with its withered grass and naked winter trees, and arrive in Steyning village.

Uncle Paddy's house links with other houses around the village's Catholic church. It had belonged to a local family, but after the death of their two sons during World War II, the house was bought by the church in the 1950s to temporarily accommodate young priests, with the spirit of promoting the Catholic faith in England.

I extend my right leg over the fence and stretch my leg, shoulder, torso, hips, buttocks and back. Some women runners tend to develop knee and foot problems because they have wider hips, but I don't fall into that category since I have narrow hips and am rather tall. Do I run the Steyning full marathon, or do I just go for the half-marathon? I screw up my face. I wasn't expecting an early menopause.

The sun has risen, and everything becomes clearer. I go through the garden and pass an old weeping willow tree. Next to the entrance some ceramic gnomes with mocking smiles welcome me. The light reflects on the gravel path, projecting a golden glow like the famous yellow brick road in the story of the Wizard of Oz.

I look in my bumbag for the keys and take out a Kleenex. I dry my forehead and hold the keys, but my body doesn't respond. Blood builds up in my hands and I can't get the key in the lock. Am I ready to go in? I sit down on the step like I used to as a child and take a deep breath. I close my knees together, cross my arms and rest my chin on them. A few houses down, a gardener prunes a leafless tree.

When I was eleven years old, Uncle Paddy left quite suddenly for his first long stay in Malaysia, helping at Catholic schools in poor neighbourhoods. Maybe it was a way to feel useful. To expiate his sins. I don't know. He had regrets about something, but he never told me what he felt guilty about.

A few months ago, he knocked on my door without warning. He had come back to stay. And now, also without warning, he has left again. The gnomes look at me, laughing at me. I get up and stretch my back. The gardener has disappeared.

I unlock and open the door and flip the light switch. A faint light comes on. I haven't been in this house since Mum passed away. The interior feels smaller than I remembered. I take off my trainers and step on a letter on the floor. It's from the bank. I pick it up and put it in my bumbag. A pungent smell of old house wraps around second-hand furniture: an oval table with marks and scratches, two wicker chairs, a shabby sofa and a metal shelf loaded with faded books.

I run my finger over the surface of the shelf. There is dust on it. An old photo in an even older frame brings a smile to my face. It was the last summer camp that Uncle Paddy, Katherine and I spent together before Katherine left for Ireland. Mum came to pick us up on the last day.

I sit on the sofa and it creaks. I was eleven years old and Katherine thirteen. I'm holding on to Uncle

Paddy's arm and he's smiling proudly. I'm squinting against the summer sun and my face is full of freckles that match the colour of my red hair. The truth is that it's not a very flattering picture. On the other hand, Katherine is very pretty. A doll in the body of a half-finished woman. One of her shoulders is more raised than the other as if the photographer had caught her by surprise and she wanted to sneak away. And three feet away from Katherine, Mum is standing with the car keys in her hand, clearly unaware that the picture is being taken. I bring the frame closer to my chest and my heart shrinks.

I go into the kitchen. On the counter, two dry teabags are withering on a spoon. The intermittent sound of drops of water hitting dirty dishes mixes with a strong odour of fried food and smelly rubbish. I wash the dishes, then take the rubbish out to the street and throw it in the bin. The gnomes are still there, laughing at me.

When I go back into the house, an alarm goes off in my mind and presses on my chest. My eyes fly from the dishes to the teabags. Something isn't right. I bend down and touch crumbs on the floor. Then I jump up. My T-shirt is damp from sweat and causes a chill in my back, and my neck tightens. I look for Sergeant Jones' card in my wallet, get the number right on the third try and put my mobile phone to my ear, where it trembles against my cheek.

'Sergeant Jones speaking.'

The words pour out of my mouth. 'I need your help.'

'Who is this?'

'It's Megan Evans, Patrick Brady's niece.'

There's a pause at the other end of the line. 'Are you all right?'

'Yes. Yes, I'm fine.' But my voice is shaking.

'What can I do for you?'

I take a deep breath and cross my arm over my chest as if to hold myself so I don't fall.

'I just got to my Uncle Paddy's house and it's all a mess.'

'Did you go to the house alone?'

'Yes.'

'Does your husband know?'

'No.'

'A friend, perhaps?' Sergeant Jones insists.

'Not yet,' I reply.

'Have you not contacted the funeral director either?'

He has too many questions.

'Not yet. I'm waiting to talk to my sister.'

'I don't understand. Why do you need my help?' he asks in a confused voice.

'My uncle's house is a mess.'

'Mrs Evans, please explain.'

'Well, there are dirty dinner plates and crumbs on the floor—'

'And that's a disaster?' he cuts me off.

'Are you not going to help me?'

'Help you with what?'

'My uncle left his house in a hurry.' Sergeant Jones doesn't answer, but I persist. 'Don't you think it's strange that he died in his car?'

'He shouldn't have gone out at night. He was elderly.'

'That's what I'm asking myself. Why did he go out at night? He never drives after dark. Nor does he like to drive alone.' Aren't these enough reasons to be suspicious? My mouth is dry as I wait for his reply.

'I honestly don't know,' Sergeant Jones says. 'But the medical report says the cause of death was respiratory arrest.'

I shake my head. 'Sergeant Jones, my uncle would never have gone out after dark, and he wouldn't have left the dishes dirty either.'

'I understand perfectly. I really do. This is a very difficult time for you. Look, I suggest you contact your sister or a friend. Talk to your family and call the funeral director.'

'No, you don't understand. My Uncle Paddy would never, ever, have gone out at night in the middle of dinner, let alone in his car. Don't you find that strange?'

Sergeant Jones says nothing for a few seconds. When he speaks again, his voice has lost its patient tone.

'And that's your hypothesis?'

'Yes,' I answer resoundingly, 'that is my hypothesis. And as I said, the house is a mess.'

'Look, I have another one. What if maybe, just maybe—' he repeats these last two words more slowly '—your uncle went out in the evening because he forgot something he needed for dinner?'

I press my mobile phone harder to my ear and stress every word. 'I would say that my uncle never went out in his car after dark.'

'And I repeat that your Uncle Paddy died from a respiratory arrest. Mrs Evans, you have to accept facts.'

'Are you raising your voice to me?'

I hang up, sigh deeply and the air whistles through my teeth in protest.

9

Tuesday, 10 January 2006
Time: 5.51 p.m.

IN THE FRONT window of my friend Sophie's charity shop, a young couple is trying out a second-hand sofa. They're having a lively conversation, interspersed with laughter. I lean forward, lost in the scene. They look like Tom and me when we were in college. I swallow and look down. When did we lose the ability to laugh together?

I grab the door handle and walk into the shop, which smells like a memory chest. The racks overflow with clothes of all kinds hanging on metal hangers. Hats, handbags and wallets snake around the shelves, and shoes and sandals in different states of wear line up underneath.

A woman with a serious face slides along one hanger after another, absent-mindedly rummaging through the clothes rack. The metallic squeaking of the hangers is monotonous and annoying. I go past the woman and find my friend sitting behind the counter with a pen and a magazine.

Although Sophie and I were friends in primary school, we lost contact many years ago and only met again in the hospital seven months ago. Sophie was crying for her mother, who was dying in a cold hospital bed, and I was crying for a son who was never born. We spent a few days drinking tea in the hospital cafeteria and keeping each other company as if we had known each other all our lives. Time stopped for us. A few days later, Sophie came home without her mother, and I returned to my life without my son. Since then, I've passed by the shop from time to time and we've shared stories and secrets.

Sophie is absorbed in a crossword puzzle from some psychology magazine she likes to read.

'Hello.'

'Hi, honey,' she answers without looking up. 'Help me, it starts with the letter "a" and contains an "h". Theory that describes the long-term dynamics of relationships between human beings.'

I leave my bag on the counter and respond with a cynical tone. 'Bitterness?'

She raises her head and opens her mouth slightly. Then she takes off her silver glasses' chain and looks at me from top to bottom.

'You're not well.'

I shake my head and pout. 'Let's just say I've had better days.'

Behind me, the metal doorbell rings. The young

couple leave, and the woman from the clothes rack approaches the counter with several garments. I step aside. I blow my nose and pretend to look at the books on the shelf. Sophie charges the woman, and once the customer leaves, she closes the shop and turns off the lights in the window.

'Give me a moment, honey. I have to call Paul to come and pick me up a little later.'

I nod. 'How is Paul?'

'In good shape.' She smiles mischievously. 'With a bigger and bigger belly, but in love with me.' Her eyes light up like two little blue buttons, and her cheeks swell to form a round face with a double chin. 'He got his contract renewed at the school bus company. The children love him,' she says as she touches her engagement ring.

I force a smile. I've never liked Paul, although Sophie doesn't have to know that. I hope she's not wronged this time.

Sophie and Paul have a cloyingly sweet conversation. I am still standing. My neck is stiff and my head hurts. Sophie hangs up and looks at me again. Her face changes and becomes serious like mine.

'Tom again? You look like you've seen a dead man.'

'My Uncle Paddy…'

'Yes?'

'Is dead.'

'Come here.' She grabs the magazine, pen and glasses and indicates for me to follow her. 'Whatever it is, tell me now.' Then she takes my hand, like I'm a little girl, and leads me into the small office. 'Sit here and tell me what's going on.'

I take off my scarf and my jacket and tell her what happened. The police, the car, my uncle.

She nods silently. 'And your sister?'

I get up, cross my arms and take a deep breath. 'I have no idea. I've lost count of how many times I've called her.'

'And Tom?'

I keep quiet for a while, a long and heavy while, and finally answer in a whisper. 'He's in Belfast. I haven't told him yet.'

'What?'

'I know, I know.' I repeat more slowly, 'I know.' I stare at nothing and open up to my friend. 'I don't know whether I want him to come back.'

Sophie's face shrinks like my heart. 'Is it that bad?'

'Yes. No. I don't know.' I sit on the chair again, hands under my arms, and my words deflate in the air. 'It's as if I don't have any energy left to go on with this relationship.'

'But it's over now, isn't it?'

'I guess.' I make a sour face.

'It's okay.'

Sophie knows when not to insist. We're silent for a while. The office is as small as a postage stamp. I notice the photo frame in my bag.

'Sophie.' I stare at her. 'Someone had dinner with my uncle the night he died.'

Sophie opens her eyes more. 'Who?'

'That's what I'd like to know. There were two dirty dinner plates.'

She thinks about it. 'What if he had a salad on one plate and the main course on the other?'

I lean my head slowly to one side. 'That is not possible. I've never seen my uncle eat on two plates. He is too humble.'

'Have you told the police?'

'No. I washed the dishes and organised the house a bit. I didn't think about it at the time. But they told me that there are no signs of a "criminal act",' I say.

'And you think there are signs of a criminal act?'

'I'm not saying there are. All I'm saying is that my uncle went out at night, got into his car and died of an asthma attack. It doesn't make sense.' I fan myself with my hands. 'Could you give me some water, please?'

Sophie leans over to me as if to say something, but stands up and brings me a glass of water. 'Here. Would you like some aspirin?'

'Yes, two.' I pull out a handkerchief and dry my forehead.

'What's with all the sweating?'

'Mother Nature doing her own thing.'

'So soon?' she asks, raising her voice.

I take the aspirin and swallow the water so fast that I hurt my throat. 'And the asthma attack thing doesn't add up.' I put the glass on the table.

'I have an idea.' She turns on the computer, lifts her fingers and says to me in a TV commercial voice, 'With the internet and these fat little fingers we are going to look for answers.'

'What are you looking for?'

'Searching for information on asthma.' She reads aloud with the tone of a presenter from the news. 'Asthma is a disease of the respiratory system characterised by chronic inflammation of the airway.'

'I already tried that. Besides, it doesn't help me,' I interrupt her. 'I didn't know my uncle had asthma. Dr Brown mentioned an intermittent asthma from the cold or something like that.'

'Okay, let's see.' She reads on. 'Here it is. Intermittent asthma appears less than once a week with night-time symptoms less than twice a month.'

'Still no use to me. Suppose Uncle Paddy knew he had asthma. Why didn't he leave the house with his inhaler?'

'Maybe it didn't happen very often.'

'Exactly.'

'What do you think of this? Here they talk about unstable or chaotic asthma: it has no apparent reason or cause.'

No apparent reason? I scratch my head.

'But there must be a reason. Look for extreme causes of asthma or something like that.'

My hands are sweating. Sophie is so close to the screen that it looks like she's going to eat it. She types greedily.

'Bingo! Here's something. Emotions don't cause asthma, but strong emotional reactions such as laughing, crying or sighing can cause symptoms, especially if the asthma is not controlled.'

'Let me see.'

She moves aside, picking up her magazine and her pen, and now I'm the one devouring the screen.

'An emotional reaction can trigger an asthma attack.' I run my finger over the screen as if I were reading the lines of a newspaper article. 'If not controlled in time, it can lead to death.'

Death?

Sophie screams out of the blue, 'Attachment!'

I almost jump out of the chair. My heart seems to come out of my mouth.

'"Attachment" is the theory that describes the long-term dynamics of relationships between human beings.' Excitedly, she fills in her crossword puzzle.

'You scared me to death.' I take a big breath of air and breathe some life into my poor heart.

'I'm sorry, honey.' She looks at me with soft eyes. 'I know you're not in a good place.' She puts her hand on my shoulder. 'I'll ask Paul to stop by your uncle's house tomorrow and we'll give you a hand with his things. If you want, you can donate some of his things to the shop.'

I nod, but my mind is elsewhere.

What or who caused such a strong emotional reaction in my uncle that he collapsed and died?

10

Tuesday, 10 January 2006
Time: 7.17 p.m.

WHEN I GET HOME, I find a package with my name on it left on the doorstep. I pick it up and open the door, then hang up my jacket, scarf and bag in the hall. I approach the mirror at the entrance; there are black bags under my eyes. I straighten my back and pat my cheeks to get the colour back. Who am I trying to fool? I breathe a weak sigh and drag my feet to the drinks cabinet, a dark lacquered wooden globe with a vintage look. Tom gave me the globe with the broken promise of travelling more often together. I put my fingers on the handle and open it like a broken egg. It's loaded with bottles for the dinners we used to have with friends. I take a bottle of Cointreau, a French liqueur made from orange peel, and pour myself a glass.

One of my friends was in the habit of having Cointreau for dessert. I haven't seen any of them since I left the hospital. I asked them not to come to see me, and then I was disappointed when all I got from them was some flowers and a frivolous letter of condolence. I wish my friends had come anyway. I squeeze the glass harder. But they didn't. I take another drink and the liqueur burns my throat.

I open the package. These are my new pink trainers with apple-green trim. They have shock absorbers on the sides and are designed for long-distance running.

Someone knocks at the door, but I'm not expecting anyone at this hour. Through the peephole I see Oliver. He must have seen the lights on in the dining room. It's not a good time, but I shrug my shoulders and open the door.

'What are you up to?' His voice is sad, and his eyes are sadder.

Oliver has changed since Amy's death. It even seems like he's lost some of his great height. He's wearing a sweatshirt as frayed as his appearance. On the left side of the sweatshirt there's a patch with the number seventy-seven sewn over his heart.

'Oliver, I'm busy.'

'I see.' He stares at the glass in my hand.

Do I let him in or not? My fingers drum on the glass. I've told him no so many times … although he isn't to blame for anything.

'Come on in. You want a drink?' I turn around and go to the drinks cabinet without a reply.

'I'm sorry about your uncle. Margie told me.'

'Margie says a lot of things. Cointreau?'

'Is it strong?'

A half smile escapes my lips and I nod.

'A double then. Is Tom…?'

'On a trip. Tom is on a trip.' I clear my throat and continue. 'Make yourself at home. It's not the first time you've been here.'

I reach out to give him his glass. He sits down on the sofa slowly and says, 'It's the first time I've been here without Amy.'

I pretend that my stomach is not shrinking and fake a frozen smile.

'We don't have Tom to make us one of his dinners either. Cheers.' I clink his glass.

Oliver takes a drink. Neither of us says anything. There is a silence, long and intense. He looks around the dining room as if remembering the time when he and Amy had dinner with us. My throat tightens. It's too painful to hear Oliver talk about his wife like a broken record.

'What are those trainers?'

His question loosens my neck. 'I've started running again.'

'Really?'

'I'm preparing for the marathon in Steyning this spring.'

'Well, you're celebrating the victory too early.'

I sit still with a rigid gaze. Am I ready to re-establish this old neighbourly relationship? The white of his cheeks turns pink.

'I'm sorry, that was a bad joke. It's not like me.'

Since Amy was killed, I've seen Oliver cry, scream, laugh and cry again in a matter of minutes. It's not fair to judge him.

'How is your son Jamie doing?' I ask.

'Good, good. I talked to him a while ago. He's with Amy's parents. Let's just say that at this point his grandparents are better company than I am.'

'What about you and everything then?'

He blinks quickly and looks down. 'I'm off work. The school found a cover teacher for the time being.'

I feel the need to get up and approach him, but I restrain myself.

'Oliver, it's been more than seven months.'

'I know, but I miss her so much.'

'I understand.' My throat is a tangle of knots.

'No, you can't understand.' His voice is harsh. 'I miss her, I want her to come back, and you, on the other hand … I know you want Tom to go.'

His comment is sharp, like a Judas dagger that slowly pierces your back. He puts his glass down hard on the table, raises his arms and grabs his head in a frustrated attempt to rip it off to stop thinking. His hands are big and masculine, and his torso, in the light, appears strong and virile. I know that in another time we could have been the ones to blame, in some other story. Now it would be out of spite. This conversation is going nowhere.

'Oliver, I have things to do.' I cross my arms.

He takes a deep breath and swallows. I study his Adam's apple as it goes up and down.

'I'm sorry, I was rude.' His voice sounds sad again.

I sigh, uncross my arms and drop my shoulders. When you run, the physical pain can be immediate, intense and unbearable. When it's gone, you forget. On the other hand, the pain of the heart is just the opposite – when it comes, you never imagine how much more it will hurt with time. I close my eyes and evoke Tom in my thoughts. There is no answer. The silence between Oliver and me is as disturbing as a premonition.

'Megan, I have to ask you something.'

I don't say anything, just lean back, keeping my distance. Oliver pauses as if choosing his words very carefully.

'You and Amy liked to meet for a drink, as good friends.'

I put one hand to my forehead. We were definitely not friends.

'Well, we were neighbours.' I confirm the obvious.

'Yes, yes, I know. Amy always told me how nice your company was.'

A thread of acid begins to rise in my throat.

His heel strikes the ground nervously, and he looks down at his wedding ring and says in a distant tone, 'I think she had a lover.'

'A lover?' I repeat, pretending to be surprised as I run my hand through my hair.

'Yes, someone she was seeing behind my back.'

'And how did you come to that conclusion after seven months?' I ask with a certain amount of suspicion and curiosity. 'You never mentioned it before.'

'I don't know. It's just a hunch.'

'Oliver, look, now is not a good time for me, with my uncle's funeral.'

I get up and take my glass and his and go to the kitchen. I feel his eyes on my back. I would like to turn around and look him in the eye. I can't.

'Did you know anything?' he says in an accusatory, unsure tone.

I open the dishwasher and automatically put the glasses inside. 'Oliver, wake up. Amy is no longer with us. Does it matter?'

'I need to know.' His voice is getting stronger.

I find my courage and turn around. 'Stop it, Oliver.'

'Please.'

'You come to my house after more than half a year to ask me if your late wife slept with other men?'

'I didn't say other men.' He stands up.

'We'd better leave it there, okay?'

He covers his face with his hands and sobs in silence. I hesitate for a moment, then approach him.

'Amy was beautiful, active, ambitious and had a wonderful personality. That's the way you should remember your wife.'

He listens to me and regains his composure. 'Will you give me the bottle as a present?' he asks.

'Okay. I have more in the drinks cabinet.'

I hold the bottle up to him and offer him a tissue, but his eyes are dry.

'Oliver, maybe not today, but tomorrow you have to start thinking about your child. And you also have to think that whatever good or bad decisions Amy made in the past, they stay there, in the past.' The words come out of my mouth without meaning to. He stares at me for a few seconds with a questioning face. He opens his mouth, closes it, then shakes his head. 'You'd better go, Oliver. I have a lot to do. We'll talk again soon.'

I usher him out and close the door on him before he asks any more uncomfortable questions.

11

Tuesday, 10 January 2006
Time: 8.02 p.m.

MINUTES LATER, the home phone rings. It's not Katherine, it's the funeral director, confirming that the funeral will be on Sunday. There will be no wake. It will be better that way. I say yes to everything with an apathetic tone while playing with the texture of the curtain in the dining room. It's a dull straw-coloured velvet. When spring comes, I'll get some more cheerful curtains. Well, if I still live here. Maybe a pastel blue that contrasts with the old wooden furniture and gives the dining room some life. The window frames a picture of naked trees over a dim light that dissipates the darkness of the night. The night has the same colour as last night, and the night before. And the night before that. And in the dark, a greyish shadow moves restlessly in the emptiness of the street.

I freeze. The strange silhouette moves awkwardly to

the front door. I pull the curtain closed and hide behind it. Isn't that the same silhouette that appeared last night, when I found my broken watch?

I try to find Oliver's number in my phone. My fingers are shaking.

'Yes?' he answers.

'Look out the window. Quickly. Do you see a man out there?' The words rush out of my mouth and my heart rumbles in my chest.

'What?'

'Look outside in the street.' I raise my voice. 'There's someone in front of my house.'

There are noises on the other end of the line as Oliver goes to look. I press my fist against my chest as if to slow down my heartbeat.

'Megan, I don't see anyone.'

Using the curtain as a shield, I peek through the window very carefully. My right hand strangles the phone as if I'm holding on to a cliff so I don't fall. The strange silhouette has disappeared.

'Megan?'

I take a deep breath and keep the air inside until I feel my heart return to its natural rhythm.

'Megan, are you still there? Are you sure you saw someone?'

I let the curtain fall.

'Of course I am.'

The front door is locked with a chain. I check all the windows in the house. They are also closed. I take the broken watch from the sideboard. It shows 6.47 on 8 January – Sunday night. The Victorian clock on the dining room wall strikes eight. I pass the watch from one hand to the other. Was it the same man who appeared yesterday? Is someone watching me? What for? Is my imagination playing tricks on me? I put the watch back in the sideboard, then go up to my room and lock the door. Should I call Tom? Or should I call the police? What would I tell them? That a strange silhouette is watching me at night? I shake my head. They'd take me for a madwoman. I shrug my shoulders and tighten the knot in my dressing gown. I'd better not call anyone. I'm alone in this.

12

Wednesday, 11 January 2006
Time: 8.32 a.m.

SIX MILES, a shower and a good breakfast was just what I needed to put my thoughts together. If there's any connection between my broken watch, the visit of a stranger and my uncle's death, I can only think of one way to identify it: find out what Uncle Paddy did in the last hours before his death. First, I'll visit Dad, and then I'll talk to Father Jonathan.

When I go out, Oliver is sitting on the step of his house with his head back, looking at the overcast sky. His mouth forms a small circle from which grey smoke emanates. I come closer, but he doesn't notice my presence. He's wearing the same T-shirt as yesterday. He's holding a cigarette between his fingers that's about to die out, and in his other hand a large cup of coffee. A few metres away from him, I raise my eyes to the spot in the sky where he's looking.

'The temperatures are dropping again,' he says in a laconic voice. His gaze is still fixed on nothing.

'Sorry for being so abrupt yesterday. I'm not in a good place.'

He lowers his head, and his eyes are inexpressive. He blinks slowly and takes a long puff on the cigarette.

'Welcome to the club.' He breathes out the grey smoke and his face blurs. 'Thank you for the liqueur.'

'You don't have to thank me.'

'Where are you going?'

'To see my father.'

'You're not working today?'

'I've asked for a few days off. I'm busy with my uncle's funeral. What's your plan?'

'I'm going to see my wife.' And he lights up another cigarette.

'I understand.'

Amy came to the right place, but on the wrong day. She arrived late and death took her away. It was her own fault. Had she arrived a day earlier, Oliver and I would still be living in ignorance. Now we're both in pain. Cold air crosses between us and I brush away a lock of hair that falls on my cheek. I choose my words very carefully.

'I just wanted to tell you that, if you need help, if you need someone to help you organise Amy's things … you know what I mean … tell me and I'll give you a hand.'

His face remains indifferent. I play with the strap of my bag, looking at it while waiting for an answer that doesn't come. 'Well, see you.'

His eyes move and he looks at my feet. 'Wait, weren't those trainers for running?'

What kind of question is that? He's changed so much.

'Oliver, I have to go, okay?' I turn around and keep walking.

'Don't be late,' he calls after me.

A gust of cold air comes over me. I reach the corner and slow down. The sky looks like a grey dome, an oppressive prison. Poor Oliver. It's better for him not to know the real reason for his wife's death, or he'd never be able to forgive her.

13

Wednesday, 11 January 2006
Time: 9.04 a.m.

DAD HAS BEEN LIVING at Lavender Lodge for almost a year now, since Alzheimer's prevented him from leading a normal life. Tom convinced me that it was the best thing for everyone, and Katherine didn't object either. Fortunately, Dad has stopped asking how much longer he'll be staying here.

Did Uncle Paddy visit Dad before he died? I swallow and walk over to the counter. Nobody is there. At the end of the corridor, a black nurse with plump arms and thick curls is pulling a trolley with small white plastic cups.

'We're short-staffed,' she explains in a slow voice as she approaches.

One of the wheels keeps catching and knocking the ground.

'I understand,' I reply.

'No, you don't understand. One sick leave and two maternity leaves in one week.' She sighs. 'Who can get pregnant in a place like this?'

I look at her, not knowing what to reply. 'I'd like to see my father, Mr Hudson.'

'Did you ask at reception?'

'Looks like no one is there.'

'We're short-staffed,' she repeats, and grunts something unintelligible. 'Besides, it's breakfast time. Do you have an appointment with your father so early today?'

'Yes. Well, not today. Monday.' I put the strap of my bag over my shoulder; now it touches my neck. 'An unexpected family matter came up and I couldn't make it.'

'You cancelled?

'No. An unexpected family issue arose,' I repeat.

'Then you cancelled.' She confirms the obvious with a slight nod.

'I guess so.'

She looks me up and down. 'Well, that's okay.' She lifts her double chin towards a notebook on the counter. 'Write down the day and the person you're visiting, sign there in the register and follow me.'

I do as she instructed, then follow her and the trolley. Two corridors later, she stops. 'There's your father.' She gestures to the end of a third corridor leading to the dining room.

I pass through double doors that transport me to another time, as if I were entering a sepia-coloured painting from another era: a quartet of men playing cards by the window overlooking the street, a group of women with impassive faces doing crochet while watching TV, and some nurses collecting their breakfast dishes. The only laughter you can hear comes from an American television programme. A nurse is cutting an apple for an old man, and another straightens the hair of an old woman holding a doll.

Dad is sitting with his back to me, alone, looking through the window overlooking the garden.

I go over and put my hand on his shoulder. 'Hi, Dad.'

He turns and I see that he's holding a shoebox in his hands. He looks at me with empty, dark, sea-coloured eyes.

'I'm Megan, your daughter.'

The air is mixed with the smell of food and the hum of low conversations between the residents and the nurses. Small cracks open at the corner of Dad's lips and let out a smile that touches my soul. I kiss him on his cheek.

'How are you, Dad?'

His smile fades. 'You're late.'

'I'm sorry I couldn't come to see you on Monday.'

'Monday? What day is today?'

'Wednesday.'

'Wednesday,' he repeats hesitantly.

'Dad, what's in that shoebox?'

'I don't know.'

I sit down and pull up my chair to be closer to him.

'I need to talk to you. It's important.'

He nods, although I'm not sure he's having a good day.

'What number comes before thirty-nine?' I ask.

He thinks and answers. 'Thirty-eight.'

'Before sixty-five?'

'Sixty-four.'

I put my hand on his. 'Uncle Paddy is no longer with us.'

I notice my reflection in the windowpane. My eyes are swollen, with dark circles underneath. I need more than a run, a shower and a good breakfast. Dad's expression is empty again. Meditative, perhaps. He puts the shoebox on the windowsill while he watches the wind tearing the few leaves from the tree in the garden.

'Did he go back to Malaysia?'

'No. He won't be visiting again. Was he with you on Sunday?'

He shakes his head. 'I don't remember saying goodbye to him.'

Dad looks at the tree and I look at him. I sigh and let a long silence pass.

'Dad, what's in that shoebox?' I ask again.

'I don't know.'

'Can I open it?'

'It's not mine.'

'Well then, I'll open it.'

My father watches me taking a curious look at the box. I reach in and find a key ring in the shape of a rabbit.

'Dad, where did you get this key ring from?'

'I don't know. Caroline?'

'Who?'

'She's pregnant. She's not coming any more.'

'And this notebook full of scribbles?'

'It's mine. To make shopping lists.'

I keep digging. A roll of undeveloped photos, an inhaler, a rusty coin. 'An asthma inhaler? Is this Uncle Paddy's?'

'I don't know,' he replies. 'It's an inhaler.'

'Look at this, a navy-blue shoelace, a small video-camera tape, a postcard from Devon…'

I turn it over. It's addressed to a Lizzie. I put it back in the box. There's also one of Tom's watches.

'What is Tom's watch doing here?'

Dad's eyes are lost through the window.

'Dad, are you listening to me?'

'The tree is withering,' he says in a languid voice.

'Trees don't wither. They lose their leaves.'

'That tree is withering,' he insists. 'It's old.'

'Dad, where did you get Tom's watch from?'

I keep looking in the box and find one of my earrings too. Dad is still in his own world.

'I asked the new nurse, that young Indian boy, to cut a healthy branch and give it to me.'

'Dad, there's one of my hoop earrings too. Where's the other one?'

'He said yes, but I haven't seen him around the past few days.'

I stop and look up. Dad is nostalgic.

'Tell me, what do you want a tree branch for?'

'The tree is dying. I want to keep a branch as a memory. I want to remember that it was here, alive, with us.'

I get a lump in my throat. I should bring Dad home

to spend time with me, now that Tom is more absent. I look for a handkerchief in my bag and blow my nose.

'Dad, Uncle Paddy has passed away.'

The expression on his face becomes taciturn. 'Passed away?'

I nod with a long, 'Yes.' He remains pensive, as if having an inner dialogue with himself. I search in his lost gaze for my father, an ounce of sanity. He raises his right hand, stares at me, then points his finger at me, giving me instructions.

'Don't say anything to Mum. I'll talk to her.'

The knot in my throat becomes a ball of sadness so big that it doesn't let me swallow. I get up, put the film and videotape in my bag and kiss him goodbye. My voice is a whisper.

'You'll have your moment to talk to Mum. See you soon.'

I leave Tom's watch and my earring in the shoebox. Dad won't forget about me.

'When will you be back?'

'Soon.'

I walk through the dining room with quick steps, holding my hand to my throat in an attempt to suppress my sorrow. I look for the bathroom. Once I enter, and I'm alone, my eyes – which have been like cracked water reservoirs for the last two days – overflow and rivers of tears run down my cheeks to my lips. They taste of salt; they taste of me.

I will not forget the memory of my family either. Uncle Paddy might still be alive if he hadn't got into his car.

14

Wednesday, 11 January 2006
Time: 10.47 a.m.

I GO TO THE CHURCH, hoping to get a glimpse into the last hours of my uncle's life and find the reason that drove him to leave his house at night.

Through the windows of the church, the candlelight zigzags like shingles. I pass through the thick, old wooden doors and go into the darkness. My eyes settle into the half-light. On the left is an ochre-coloured tin fountain with holy water. I put my hand in the cold water and bless myself. A strong smell of incense pervades the church. I pass through a chain of sober mahogany benches. The walls are loaded with crosses, crucifixes, chalices, angels and images of saints. At the front, decorated with yellow carnations, is the altar with Jesus hanging from his cross. His eyes watch me so realistically that no matter what angle I look from, the image of Jesus Christ follows me with his gaze. I join my hands and from my lips comes a prayer that disappears in a sigh. In a corner to the right, the confessional is hidden. A dark wooden box, almost black, where, as a child at Sunday Mass, I used to confess my sins to the priest. I lick my dry lips. Then a hoarse voice pronounces my name and I wake up from my thoughts.

'Megan, my daughter. Is that you?'

Father Jonathan approaches me with short steps. The years have punished him with a great excess of weight, disguised by a black cassock and a white collar that can no longer do its job of lifting his neck.

'Father Jonathan, do you remember me?'

'My daughter, how could I not?' He puts his palms together and raises them to his chin in a rehearsed prayer. 'Let me think. Almost ten years have passed. I'm sorry to see you again in such sad circumstances.' I swallow and he continues, 'I never had a better sacristan than your Uncle Paddy.' He looks down and shakes his head several times. 'Come with me.' He takes my hand. 'You look tired.'

The bench creaks when we sit down.

'Father Jonathan, I would like to ask you something about my uncle.'

'Don't worry, my daughter. I know this is a difficult time for you and your sister Katherine. I confirmed with the funeral director the Mass for this Sunday. We will not delay this grief any longer.' His voice sounds serene and contrasts with my concerns.

'I need you to clarify certain things for me. I'm a little confused.'

He squeezes my hand. 'On Sunday we will give your

uncle the goodbye he deserves.' He makes a half-finished, sad smile and I can see the marks of the collar in his chubby jaw. I withdraw my hand.

'Father Jonathan, don't you find his sudden death strange? It doesn't make sense.'

'It does in God's eyes.'

'Yes… When was the last time you saw my uncle?'

He leans back, thoughtful. 'Sunday.'

'Was he with you?'

He hesitates. 'He was not at Sunday Mass.'

'But did he talk to you?'

'I don't remember.'

'You don't remember whether you spoke to him on Sunday?'

'Well, I do remember. We talked about little things. Nothing of interest.' He clears his throat. 'Some Sunday afternoons he would come home with me for tea. He didn't come this time and I thought that maybe he was tired.' He looks at the cross. 'God keep him in his bosom.' He blesses himself.

'I understand.'

Do I really understand? The candles on the altar flicker nervously. I lift my head towards the image of Jesus as if waiting for him to answer me.

'And you didn't talk about anything?' I persist.

'Talk about what?'

'I don't know, something. Anything.'

His smile fades. 'Why are you asking me this?'

'When he died, Uncle Paddy was out in his car at night. Do you know why?'

'My child, you must accept the circumstances and have faith.'

'No, Father, I mean, if Uncle Paddy didn't have tea with you because he was tired, I don't understand why he went out in his car at night.'

There is a longer pause. Father Jonathan looks at Jesus Christ, raises his hand and puts his index finger in his mouth. When he speaks, his voice is hoarser. 'He never mentioned to me that he was tired. As he didn't come to my house, I thought he'd be at his, resting. Maybe he forgot something and went out in his car—'

'What?' I interrupt him.

I cross my arms and hunch my shoulders as if I were small for a moment. How many times have I asked myself that question? But nobody gives me an answer.

Father Jonathan breaks the silence. 'Did you collect your uncle's belongings?'

'Yes, on Monday. I also spoke to the coroner.'

'And what did the coroner say?'

'I don't remember the medical term he used. It was an asthma attack that escalated to cardiac arrest due to lack of oxygen. It's rare, but not unknown. What reason could my uncle have had to go out at night?'

Father Jonathan's face is sullen. 'I don't know, my daughter. Only God knows. Your uncle was always a wandering soul. A soul full of energy and charisma, but also humble and discreet.'

'I agree. So discreet that nobody knows why he went out that night.'

So discreet that it cost him his life?

'God keep him in his bosom.' The priest blesses himself again.

My mobile phone rings. First ring. I don't recognise the number. Father Jonathan looks at me with surprise and disapproval. Second and third ring. I jump up and run to the front door. Fourth ring. I can't miss this call. Fifth ring. I trip over the doorstep and fall to the floor. Sixth ring.

'Hello?' I answer, breathless.

'Are you all right?'

'Yes, yes.' My right knee hurts.

'This is Sergeant Jones.'

'Yes…?'

He clears his throat. 'Two constables will be coming to your uncle's house shortly. Can you be there?'

'Yes.'

'All right.' And he hangs up.

The corners of my lips are raised in a smile. My knee no longer hurts. I try to stand up.

'Hi. Hi. Are you all right?'

Someone touches my shoulder, and my back tightens. His voice is heavy with a bit of stuttering. His hands are dirty with soil. I turn my shoulder away and raise my head. In front of me is a man wearing a gardener's overall a couple of sizes too big. He looks at me as he narrows his eyes.

'Yes, thank you.' I hesitate.

Father Jonathan approaches me and extends his hand. 'Are you all right, my child?'

I nod. 'Father, can I ask you something?'

'Of course you can.'

The gardener is staring at us, and I keep quiet.

'Peter, can you leave us alone?' Father Jonathan says.

The gardener walks away on bowed legs, moving his head from side to side with each footstep.

'Who is that?'

'Peter? He takes care of the church garden. The poor man had meningitis when he was young, and still has the innocence of a child.' He removes his collar. 'What can I do for you?'

'Will you come with me to Uncle Paddy's house?'

'Now?'

'Now,' I repeat with the same intensity with which he asked me. I put my hand near his arm, but I take it away before touching him. 'I need a second opinion.'

Father Jonathan says nothing. He blinks nervously. After a few seconds, his face relaxes. 'Let me close the sacristy.'

'Thank you.'

15

Wednesday, 11 January 2006
Time: 11.24 a.m.

FATHER JONATHAN WALKS along the pavement with his hands clasped behind his back. I try to match the slow pace of his short, clumsy steps. We turn the corner, and a police car passes by us, parking in front of Uncle Paddy's house. Once the police inspect my uncle's house, they will re-evaluate the official report. For some reason, Uncle Paddy was forced to leave his house in the middle of dinner, and the police have to find out what he was running from the night he died.

Constable Reed gets out of the car, followed by a policewoman. Sergeant Jones isn't there, and that works in my favour.

'Good morning,' both police constables say.

Constable Reed's cheeks swell with a jovial smile. His partner, a thin woman, looks even younger than him. Her complexion is the colour of white plaster and she moves confidently inside a bulletproof vest and a white shirt. She holds out her hand to me.

'I'm Constable Fiona Robertson. We'd like to take a look at your uncle's house,' she says in a determined voice.

'Of course.'

They approach the door and Father Jonathan and I follow them.

'Do you have the key?' Constable Robertson asks.

I pass between them and open the door. Constable Robertson comes in first and Constable Reed follows her. I stay behind next to Father Jonathan, by the doorway.

The police inspect the room from side to side with hawklike eyes. Constable Robertson raises her head and signals Constable Reed to go up the stairs. His steps sound dry on the wood.

'Stay there, please,' says Constable Robertson, and then she strolls into the dining room. She looks up and down as if photographing every detail in her memory. As she inspects the house, I inspect her, and next to me, Father Jonathan watches me quietly. Nobody says anything.

From the first floor, Constable Reed's steps move from Uncle Paddy's room to his bathroom and then down the stairs. He looks at his partner and shakes his head. Constable Robertson opens her eyes wider and nods her head back. What are they thinking?

I give my voice an exaggerated tone of concern. 'You can see that everything is a mess.'

Constable Robertson looks at me with catlike eyes. 'Tell me, what do you see?'

'What do you mean?' I open my eyes wider. 'Everything is a mess.'

I close my fists and tighten my arms. Father Jonathan is still at the door. He doesn't come in.

Constable Reed intervenes. 'Mrs Evans, I'm going to inspect the back garden.'

Constable Robertson doesn't say anything. She enters the kitchen, sighs with a certain apathy and opens one of the cupboards without much interest. She turns around and stands by the bench. Her pink lips contrast with her white skin. She is too beautiful to be a police constable. When Constable Reed returns from the garden, he looks at his partner and shakes his head again.

The blood stops in my hands, forcing me to move my fingers.

The police constables stand next to each other. Father Jonathan closes the entrance door, approaches me and tries to say something, but remains silent.

'We don't see anything unusual, Mrs Evans. I'm sorry,' says Constable Robertson.

'But don't you see what I see?' My voice is tinged with frustration.

'What do you see?'

I move around the dining room and point out the evidence. 'The dishes were on the table when I arrived and there were also dirty dishes in the sink.' I go over to the rug in the dining room and point to it. 'There are crumbs on the floor. I'm sure my uncle was forced to leave his house urgently.' I cross my arms while waiting for an answer. All eyes are on me.

'We see what you see,' says Constable Reed.

'And?'

'And we don't see anything out of the ordinary,' says Constable Robertson.

I tighten my gluteal muscles as if preparing for a long-distance race. I hit the ground with my foot and feel my cheeks reddening.

'And what should there be? Blood?' I ask with sarcasm.

'Calm down, Mrs Evans. We have come as you asked us to,' says Constable Reed.

'You paint my uncle as if he were not in his right mind. But you'd have to be blind…' I slowly raise my hand and wipe a drop of sweat from my forehead.

Constable Robertson hands me a tissue. What does that young woman know about menopause?

'See the chair?' she says. 'Your uncle stood up and pushed the chair away. If the chair had been lying on the floor, we would have been suspicious. Did you move the chairs?'

I shake my head and Constable Robertson continues, 'There are no utensils on the floor or plates lying around or anything that would make us think that your uncle had an altercation with anyone. Do you understand?'

'In addition,' says Constable Reed, 'the bed is made, and the bathroom is also in perfect condition.'

'So?' I ask.

'So, it's true that your uncle could have left his house on Sunday night,' says Constable Robertson.

'For what?'

'Well, I don't know. To buy something he forgot. Bread, milk…'

'Milk?' I repeat in disbelief.

'Whatever,' insists Constable Robertson. 'But he didn't run away because he was attacked or was escaping from someone. It could simply have been an oversight.'

'An oversight?' I raise my voice more.

I put the tissue in my pocket and go upstairs and check Uncle Paddy's room again. The bed is made. I go into the bathroom. Everything is in order. I lean against the door frame of the room. Could my uncle really have gone out to buy something at the last minute? I walk down the stairs slowly, with my head down. The police and Father Jonathan are still there.

'My daughter, you should be grateful that these police constables came at such short notice.'

'But, Father, don't you find it all a bit strange?'

For some reason, Father Jonathan is not on my side.

'Father Jonathan,' asks Constable Robertson, 'is there a shop nearby that's open on Sundays?'

'The petrol station is almost two miles away.'

'And what time do they close on Sundays?'

'Seven o'clock, I think.'

Constable Robertson approaches and asks me in a soft voice, 'Is it not possible that your uncle went out on Sunday night, took his car and went to the nearest petrol station to buy something before it closed?' Her catlike eyes are staring at me.

'It is possible.' Father Jonathan steps forward and nods several times as he looks at me, hoping for the same reaction.

'It's possible,' I repeat like an echo, and my voice shrinks. 'It's possible.'

I sit on the sofa as if waiting for my uncle to come through the door, surprising us all. "Here I am. I forgot to buy milk."

But Uncle Paddy won't be coming back.

It's time to go home.

What no one has yet explained to me is why there were two dirty dinner plates and not one. Who had dinner with Uncle Paddy the night he died?

16

Wednesday, 11 January 2006
Time: 12.31 p.m.

'GOOD AFTERNOON.' I put the bag with my mum's coat on the counter and show the young Indian shop assistant the tear. 'Could you fix this and dry-clean the coat?'

He takes the bag. Behind him hangs a wardrobe of jackets, coats, dinner jackets, party dresses and even a couple of wedding dresses, all covered in transparent plastic. In the corner, an old lady with spiky white hair in a purple Indian dress is working absent-mindedly at her sewing machine.

'One moment,' says the shop assistant.

He shows the coat to the old lady, who wakes up from her work and communicates in a language that in my ignorance I can only classify as being of Indian origin. The woman inspects the lining of the coat and nods.

The young shop assistant takes the bag and writes some notes on a receipt while he asks me, 'When do you want it by?'

'Before Friday if possible. I'll be away next week.' Mum's coat will bring me luck at the job interview on Tuesday.

'No problem,' he replies.

'Thank you.'

I come out of the shop and the air feels cold. Then I go to the only photo shop in the village, next to the local supermarket. The windowpanes are the same ones as when I was a child, and cold-resistant weeds grow in the corners. The shop has changed owner three times in the last twenty years, although I don't know the new owners. I push the glass door open and the jingling sound of the bell welcomes me. The shop smells of developing liquid and cheap air freshener.

'I have a camera film and a videotape to develop.'

The shop assistant looks me up and down with impudence. His big nose holds little glasses. Curly blond hair falls thickly over his round face like a bad version of *The Lion King*, and a black T-shirt with a rock band print barely covers his belly.

'You don't develop videotapes,' he says, without paying attention to me.

'Well, whatever you say.'

'This tape is old, but in good condition. They don't make these any more.'

'But can you develop it, or whatever it's called? I need the video for my parents' anniversary. It's a bit urgent,' I lie. I have the urge to know what's hidden in the video and the film I found in Dad's memory box.

The shop assistant leaves the tape on the counter. He's chewing mint-scented gum.

'I can convert it to DVD format if you want. But I have to ask a friend. I don't have a video camera that can read this tape.' His voice cuts off and his expression changes. Then he adds emphatically, 'You look familiar. I remember you.'

I take a short step backwards and tense my legs. 'Me?'

'I saw you on Monday at the police station.'

The shop assistant is much younger than he looks. A Peter Pan from a heavy-metal concert.

'What were you doing at the police station?' I say.

'Being a witness.'

'Witness to what?'

'I have an extra job at the local day-care centre. A couple of hours, before they open. Sometimes I stay with the little ones if an assistant gets sick, and play with them. My nephew is there too. I'm a cool uncle.' He raises his fist, making the horns, and his smile shows gum stuck to a row of badly shaped teeth. The size of his body hides a young man who has just finished his adolescence.

'Witness to what?' I repeat, confused.

'I saw a dead man in a car.'

My heart stops suddenly and each of his words enters my ears as dissonant notes. An echo is repeated inside me: *I saw a dead man in a car.* I put my hand to my lips and find it difficult to articulate the words.

'A dead man in a car?' I murmur more than ask.

'He wasn't breathing. I've seen it before. The heart stops, the skin tightens, but the muscles loosen, which affects the bladder and the intestines. You know what I mean. They don't have the strength to retain anything.' He pulls up his tight black jeans and speeds up his words. 'Half an hour later the ash-coloured skin darkens, and the texture is like wax, purple wax. The most important thing is the body temperature. The maths is easy: the body cools down one and a half degrees per hour. That's how the exact moment of death is determined. The only problem is gravity, since blood accumulates in the lower part of the body, leaving pale lips, and the hands swell and turn blue. Dark blue.' He swallows. 'The eyes sink, although the expression of the face doesn't change, it becomes even clearer. After several hours, rigor mortis begins.' He raises his hands to give more expression to his speech. 'The body becomes rigid as stone and the only thing to do is wait about twelve hours until the muscles relax again.' He appears thoughtful, no longer looking at me. He seems to be talking to himself. 'The police were lucky with me.' His chest swells up. 'I found him after twelve hours, so it was easier for them to get the body out of the car.'

In my throat, a corrosive bile defies gravity. My mouth fills with water and I fight the urge to vomit. I clench my fist against my stomach. What is this moron talking about? I take another step back and swallow the bile.

'Where have you seen that before?' I ask.

'What?'

'You said you'd seen it before. Where have you seen a dead man before?'

The Gothic Peter Pan swallows, and his double chin moves too. 'In the movies.' His voice is now shy.

'I'm his niece.'

'Shit, it's you.' His eyes widen.

'What did you see?'

'I told you. He was dead when I arrived. I'm sorry.' He adjusts his T-shirt and looks at me for a few seconds as if trying to read my thoughts. 'I have a photographic memory and I remember his face. Do you want to know what his face looked like?'

I don't reply. I remember my late uncle's face well. I lower my head and stand as still as a statue. Shame and curiosity fight a battle inside me. As soon as I nod, the shop assistant continues, excited.

'He had his eyes open like plates, and his face—'

'What did his face look like?' I interrupt him.

'I don't mean the face itself.' He frowns and shakes his head. 'I don't know. His mouth…'

'What about his mouth? Did someone assault him? Be clear.'

'He had his mouth half open.' His hands paint in the air an impression of Uncle Paddy's yawn, and my imagination gives colour to that picture. 'His mouth half open as if death came before he finished his last sentence. His last words.'

My body threatens to collapse, and my voice is a whisper, a thought out loud. 'Poor Uncle Paddy. Alone and looking lost into nothingness…'

'You're wrong,' the shop assistant says. 'You're

wrong, that's what I don't understand. His eyes were looking…' He stops and points his fingers while he thinks for a few seconds, as if solving a mathematical formula. 'Towards the glass on his left. He was looking to his left.'

The blood is throbbing in my temples. Was someone else in the car when Uncle Paddy died? I shrug my shoulders and look across the counter at a row of cameras of different shapes and sizes resting upside down like metal eyes examining me.

'He died of an asthma attack,' I say.

'Wow, just like in the movies.'

'It's not a movie,' I say loudly, as the doorbell rings behind me.

A young girl with a backpack enters slowly and the shop assistant assesses her from top to bottom.

'And the photos?' I try to regain his attention, and he replies without taking his eyes off the girl.

'I'm sorry for your loss.'

'When will you have the photos ready?' I ask.

'I can have them in a couple of hours. It usually costs extra, but I won't charge you.'

'Thank you. And the video?'

'I'll talk to my friend and let you know. The tape is old. There might not be anything on it.'

'Okay. I'll be back later.'

I leave the shop and head for the bus stop. I want to go back to Uncle Paddy's house before Sophie and Paul arrive to help me pack. If he was with someone that night, there must be a clue in his house.

17

Wednesday, 11 January 2006
Time: 12.58 p.m.

IT'S SLEETING. I cross the street and take shelter in the bus stop. Next to me, an old woman with a shopping trolley and a young boy with a red cap are also waiting for the bus. I pull my scarf up over my cheeks. The rain is pounding against the glass like a battalion on the march.

I open my bag and take out Uncle Paddy's wallet that the police handed over to me. I examine it from different angles without a specific purpose. There's nothing special about it. I open it and take out a few cards from the supermarket, the library and the bank. There's also a photo of my sister and another one showing me when we took our first communions. I hold the photos next to each other. All we have in common is the white dress and the uncomfortable posture. I put the wallet away, take out a handkerchief and blow my nose.

The bus arrives. I get on, pay and sit down. The smell of petrol mixes with an excess of heat and the rattling of the engine makes the trip uncomfortable and stifling. Two stops later, the old woman gets off and it's just me and the guy in the red cap for another five minutes of driving. The bus creeps along a circuit of winding grey streets towards Steyning. The rain is pounding just like my headache.

In the reflections in the window, I see that the boy in the red cap is watching me. I move my head and he looks away. I touch the stop button and get up. It has the same metallic sound as my mobile phone. The bus bell rings again. Then again, and again. The boy looks at me.

'What do you want?' I ask him irritably.

He points at me and says, 'Your phone is ringing.'

The bus doors open. I get out and put my foot in a muddy puddle. I open my bag and look for the light of my mobile phone. It's right at the bottom. The mobile keeps ringing and I catch it like a bird trying to escape. The screen shines with the name of the caller. My neck tightens and I reread the name several times as my heart starts to race.

It's Katherine!

I press the button, but I have no tactile sensation. I'm wearing my gloves. I take the phone in my left hand and pull the glove off my right hand with my teeth. I spit out the glove and it falls into the puddle.

'Katherine! Finally. I've been trying to reach you.' My words pour out like a motor in propulsion. I pick up the dirty glove and start walking to Uncle Paddy's.

'I know.'

'I don't know how many times I've called your mobile.'

'I know.'

'Yesterday I also called your work. I hope you didn't mind.'

'I know that too, but it's a little late to mind.'

'I have some bad news for you.'

'I know the bad news. Uncle Paddy has died.'

I stop suddenly. 'Yes.' The adrenaline stops surging through my body and my voice deflates. 'How did you know?' I hold my mobile with my head and shoulder so that it doesn't fall down while I'm juggling to find the keys and open the door of Uncle Paddy's house.

'My secretary passed me your message.' Her voice sounds tired, but mine becomes louder.

'And you're only calling me now?'

'The important thing is that I've called, isn't it?'

I'm speechless. Family has never been a priority for Katherine, but this time it's ridiculous. I grit my teeth as she continues, 'I didn't know Uncle Paddy was sick.'

'I don't think he *was* sick. His body was found in his car. Don't you think that's strange?'

She doesn't react. Has the line been cut?

'Katherine? Katherine, are you still there?'

'Carry on, please.'

'He was found by an idiot who needs a good wash and some clean clothes. Why would he have gone out in his car at night? You know he never drove after dark. And Katherine, when I got to his house, he hadn't even picked up the dinner plates. It was as if he'd run away from something.' There's a long silence on the other end of the line. Am I talking to myself? 'Katherine?' I'm standing in the dining room now.

'I'm still here. Tell me, did he die instantly?'

'What do you mean?'

'I mean, did he die in a car accident? Megan, you're not explaining yourself well. Can you please calm down?'

I hold my mobile more tightly and squeeze the words out slowly. 'According to the coroner's report, he died of an asthma attack caused by the cold. Apparently, it's rare but not impossible.'

'What else?'

'The shop assistant from the photo shop found Uncle Paddy in the car on Monday morning and called the police. If you want a more detailed explanation, stop by the shop and he'll enjoy telling you about the process of decomposition of a body.'

'That's not funny.'

'You said it, it's not funny. I don't understand what Uncle Paddy was doing in his car on a Sunday night, if he didn't like to drive after dark.'

Katherine is beginning to awaken from her apathy. 'Come back down to earth, Megan. Uncle Paddy lived his own life. You weren't in his head and you don't know his comings and goings.'

'His comings and goings? You're the one who has to return to earth. I've called you a lot of times. He's your uncle too.'

'I told you, I've been busy.'

I don't answer. On the other end of the line, I can

hear Katherine's breathing. She's probably biting her nails, like she did when she was a child. The family has always been too big for her. I stand at the window overlooking the street. Who was with Uncle Paddy on Sunday night? Did he stand here, in the same position as I am now, waiting for that guest? I go closer to the glass and it fogs up with the condensation from my breath. I draw little hearts. Then I take a deep breath and my voice softens. 'I'm sorry, Katherine. I'm a little nervous.'

'What are you going to do now?'

'The Mass is on Sunday. Other than that, I don't know.'

'Do you need money?'

I frown. 'It's not money that I need. There's a lot to organise.'

'I understand. Send me the number of the funeral home. I'll take care of it. Take care of yourself.'

And she hangs up before I hear myself saying, 'You too.'

I walk in a circle through the dining room, looking for any clues. An old sofa sits beside a wicker chair with a folded blanket over its arm, and next to the chair, there's a floor lamp with a dust-covered bulb. A television is on top of a console with an old video player. All very sparse.

I go into the kitchen. The cabinets are made of cream-coloured sheet metal, the cheapest thing on the market more than thirty years ago. On the wall hangs a calendar with appointments and religious events and several pen marks and crosses. In the drawers I find a set of four spoons, forks and knives. I open one of the cupboards. It's full of packs of coffee, cups of different sizes and a tin containing an open packet of biscuits. The smell is strong. The cupboard door doesn't close properly. I step down and notice a sachet of sugar lying on the floor. I pick it up with a napkin and throw it away.

Then a light comes on in my head with the intensity of fifty halogen bulbs, and my cheeks warm. I grab my mobile phone and call the police. I have the clue I was looking for.

My uncle only took sweetener.

18

Wednesday, 11 January 2006
Time: 1.27 p.m.

'STEYNING POLICE STATION. CONSTABLE COLLINS
SPEAKING.'

'Someone was at my uncle's house on Sunday night.'
The words rush out of my mouth.

'Sorry?'

My hands are sweating, and my joints are stiff. I
clear my throat and continue. 'I spoke to you on
Monday. You gave me a bag with my uncle's personal
belongings, but I can't find the inhaler. Do you
remember?'

'Megan Evans.' Her voice sounds like a teacher
taking the class register. 'In the bag are all the personal
belongings that my colleagues collected. I assume that
you also have the keys to the car?'

'You assume correctly. As it states in the medical
report, my uncle's death was caused by an asthma

attack. And, one would also like to assume that his inhaler should be with his personal belongings. Or am I wrong?'

'Hmm.' I don't know if her answer sounds like doubt or irritation. 'Would you prefer to talk to Sergeant Jones?'

'Yes, please.'

There is a pause with a background of inaudible conversations. I cross my fingers and hold my breath, then exhale and move my legs, letting the blood circulate. I straighten my back until my neck crunches. Uncle Paddy's house is stuffy.

'Sergeant Jones speaking.' Every syllable falls tiredly from his mouth.

'This is Megan Evans. We've talked several times about my Uncle Patrick, do you remember?'

'I remember that the first time we talked on the phone, you hung up on me. The second time, I sent two constables to inspect your uncle's house as you asked. How can I help you this third time?'

I ignore his sarcasm.

'I'm packing up my uncle's things and I've looked in the bag they gave me at reception on Monday, but something is missing.'

'Missing?'

'His inhaler.'

'His inhaler?' he repeats.

'Correct.' I stretch each syllable with force.

'I was present when we searched the car and made an inventory of his personal belongings. Everything is in the report: your uncle's body was taken to the funeral home, the vehicle was examined and the witness was questioned.' His voice comes to life as if he's come closer to the phone. 'Mrs Evans, your uncle had the bad luck to die in his car.'

'So that's your conclusion?'

'My conclusion is that there was no inhaler.'

'And you don't find that strange?'

'Not really.'

The heat in my cheeks is more intense. 'Don't you think it's strange that my uncle left his house that night, got into his car and was found dead several miles away from an asthma attack?'

'Mrs Evans, you're back to the same thing. I want to remind you that I sent two of my constables this morning to inspect your uncle's house as you requested. His death was from natural causes. You heard Dr Brown. I have nothing further to add.' He sighs. 'It wasn't the first case and it probably won't be the last. Possibly, he felt uncomfortable, stopped the car, the symptoms became more acute and he, unfortunately, died of a respiratory arrest. I understand that it's hard to accept the loss of a loved one, but—'

'And you don't find it strange that he went out at night without his inhaler?'

There is a silence on the other end of the line, a long, uncomfortable silence, and it seems as if I hear my own words echoing in my head.

'Mrs Evans, are you at your uncle's house now?'

'Yes, why?'

'Go to the kitchen.'

I follow his instructions.

'Open the drawers, please.'

'I've opened them before.'

'Then empty them out completely.'

I open the drawer, pick up some receipts and a couple of notebooks and dig through the papers. 'What am I supposed to be looking for?'

'You're looking for your uncle's inhaler. Can you see it?'

The initial surprise turns to shame. My body is a stone that doesn't want to move while I reply almost voicelessly, 'Yes.'

'How many are there?'

'Two. No, three. One brown and two blue. How do you—?'

'Thank you. I'm sure that if you look in the drawers in the dining room or in the bathroom, you will find more inhalers.'

'How do you know?'

'Because your uncle probably didn't have just one inhaler, Mrs Evans. People with asthma usually have several. In addition, your uncle's asthma manifested itself through changes in temperature, low temperatures. That is why we assume that he didn't think about taking his inhaler.' He stops for a moment, takes a breath and speaks more slowly. 'Something your uncle did not predict on Sunday night. That's why we also assume that he was only expecting to be out for a short time.'

I keep silent. My pulse beats in my temples as I listen to the ticking of Uncle Paddy's cuckoo clock. I tilt my head and turn my eyes towards the dining room and look at the second hand, which runs tirelessly in circles.

Circles that go nowhere. I raise my fingers and move them in the air as if trying to touch and catch a time that escapes me, and my eyes well up.

'Are you going to hang up on me again?'

'No. I…'

A tear slips down my cheek and my mobile is as heavy as a rock. A sudden headache squeezes my temples. Am I going crazy? Sergeant Jones' voice brings me back to reality.

'Look, when my father died, it was a very difficult time in my life. The doctors couldn't save him and I couldn't accept it. My mother said that it was sad to accept facts, but even sadder and more miserable to live in a parallel universe.'

His voice seems so close that I imagine I feel the air from his words brushing my cheeks.

'Mrs Evans?'

'Yes?' My voice gets stuck in my throat.

'Stop looking for a situation that does not exist. There are no culprits. Forgive me if I'm interfering in your life, but perhaps you should contact your husband, give your uncle a dignified funeral and try to move on. We will be in touch.'

'Thank you.'

And I hang up, but not abruptly. I drop my arms. The sound of a car engine approaches the house and I look through the old window. It's Sophie and Paul. I run my fingers over my eyes, erasing any trace of tears. I take out a wet wipe and wipe my face. Then I pull back my hair with a rubber band and open the door.

'Hello, darling.' Sophie gives me a warm hug and throws me a kiss.

Paul is next to her.

'Hi, Paul. Thanks for coming and helping us out.'

Paul looks at the floor and greets me back.

'Where do we start?' Sophie asks.

'Please take anything that's useful to you, and leave what isn't. If you find anything more personal, just put my name on it and put it aside.'

'Aren't you staying?'

'Do you mind if I go out just for half an hour to get some air? I need to collect some photos.'

Sophie looks into my eyes, as if she were reading an open book, and nods. 'Of course not. Take your mobile phone with you in case I need to call you.' She gives me another hug and whispers in my ear. 'We're having dinner tonight, and I'm not taking no for an answer.'

I nod with a forced smile.

I feel like I've lost a battle in a war that never existed, and suddenly I miss Tom.

19

Wednesday, 11 January 2006
Time: 2.55 p.m.

'I WAS WAITING FOR YOU.'

The shop assistant reaches under the counter and takes out a box full of envelopes with photos. He flicks through, takes out an envelope and puts it on the counter. His hand is as big and thick as his belly.

'The film is old, so some of the photos are blurred.'

'Nothing unusual?'

His thick blond curls move as he shakes his head without really understanding. 'It's a Nokia film with thirty-six photos.'

'Thank you. And the videotape?'

'You're lucky. My friend has lent me his camera for this tape, an old model. I'm going to transfer it to DVD format. I can have it ready tomorrow. The cost depends on the length of the tape.'

'Perfect.'

I pay him then put the photos in my bag, but when I get to the door of the shop, I stop for a moment. The photos were from a film I found in a box with objects my father steals and collects. Old photos that have ended up in the hands of an old man with Alzheimer's disease.

Casually, I take the envelope out of my bag and slide my hand inside it. My heart pumps from excitement, which runs freely through my veins. My senses are sharpened.

I look at the first photo: some girls swimming in a river. There are three of them. They are splashing in the water, in the distance. The colours are pale. Their inno-cent smiles fill my heart with nostalgia. I take a deep breath and swallow, then move on to the next photo. It's the same girls jumping into the river. It's summer and the sunlight diffuses part of the photo, but it's clear that they're the same girls. They might be about eleven or twelve years old. I hold the photo closer to the light, but the faces don't look familiar.

Someone opens the door and the cold wakes me up.

'Excuse me.'

I quickly put the photos away in my bag and give a polite smile. I hold the door to let in a mother with a pushchair with a little girl about three years old inside. Next to the pushchair, an older boy grabs the handle and enters with his mother.

'Come on, we'll be done soon,' she says to her son as they come in.

I stand at the door like a thief with a moral dilemma. I flick through more photos. Girls in swim-ming costumes running one after the other. Girls sitting quietly by the riverbank. Girls watching other girls jumping into the river from a tree branch. The colour resolution is not very good, and the summer clothes worn by the girls date back several decades. It looks like a school excursion or something like that. I don't recognise the place or the girls.

I turn around and walk back into the shop. There's no one at the counter. I turn to the left and see the mother struggling with her daughter, who won't keep still in the pushchair, while the shop assistant, in front of them, has his head tilted adjusting a camera and a light.

I go closer, but stop halfway. At my feet, lying face down, the older child is playing with a toy truck. He looks up with a curious expression. I raise my hand to get the shop assistant's attention.

'Sorry to bother you. Do you have the videotape?'

The shop assistant lifts his nose at the same time as he blinks.

'Didn't you want me to transfer it to DVD format?'

'Yes, but I want to see it first, if possible. It will only take a moment.'

My eyes meet the mother's, asking for permission. She's young with short straight hair and dark brown eyes. I feel the plastic truck passing by and running over one of my feet.

'You go,' says the mother, holding a comb and some coloured ribbons. 'I still have to do her hair.'

'Thank you.'

The shop assistant comes over and puts the video camera on top of the counter. He hooks up some cables, opens the camera and puts in the tape.

'This little screen will show you the video. Here's play, and here's stop. It's like a children's toy. You got it?'

'I'll let you get back to your other customer.' I gesture with my head to the left.

I leave the envelope with the photos on the counter and take out a pair of headphones from my bag. I put my fingertips on the flap and check that the shop assistant is busy with the other customer and her daughter. Then I lift the flap and take out all the photos. I quickly go through them as if flipping through the pages in a book before buying it. There are girls posing in front of the camera, making faces. Photos with one girl, a duo, a trio and girls posing in a group. Girls drying each other's hair with towels. Girls laughing, others serious. Happy girls and laughing girls. Girls with the bodies of children and other girls entering puberty, but all with the same halo of innocence. Girls here and girls there. Girls and more girls.

I found the film along with the videotape in Dad's memory box. That doesn't necessarily mean they had a direct relationship, does it? The videotape is old too. Maybe Dad can give me an explanation. I doubt it though. I put the photos back in my bag and put my headphones on. I have to know what's on the video before that jerk transfers it onto a DVD. I'd die of shame if anything unusual were to appear.

I move my head; the child is now standing almost beside me. He's as tall as the counter and is playing with the truck on the glass. I try to bring the camera closer to me, but I can't. The cable is too short. I bend over in an uncomfortable position and bite my lip while my eyes focus on that small window.

I hit *play* and it feels like the same button is pressing hard on my chest. Am I ready for what I'm about to see? The child comes closer to me with his bloody truck and I lose my concentration. I look up, but his mother is too busy in the background manoeuvring to get her daughter straight as a doll for the photo. A couple of seconds later I hear the sound come on, and the screen lights up in grey with a thousand ants walking around. I stop breathing for a moment and my skin starts to bristle.

The child looks at me shamelessly. I'm more interesting than his little truck. I cover the screen with my hand and look at him defiantly. He doesn't move. Suddenly, a tune bursts out of it and my heart shrinks as if I need to hide from danger. My hand covers the screen, but my ears hear a song: 'Girl, You'll Be a Woman Soon'. I bite my lip harder, but I feel no pain. The child stares at my hand. His gaze is intense and as curious as mine. I concentrate on the lyrics of the song.

I stand straighter and try to move the camera towards me. Impossible. I lean back and move my fingers from the screen. The child has left the truck on the ground. He has his hands resting on the counter at the height of his mouth and is looking directly at the camera screen. I get an idea. I move my fingers slightly, trying to look through a window with grids. Nothing. I only see shadows. I can't see what's behind the song. Then the child runs away. This is my chance.

'Everything okay?'

I leap up, bathed in a cold sweat, and close the screen quickly. 'Yes, yes.'

The shop assistant looks at the camera and frowns when he sees that the screen is closed. The doorbell rings and a couple enters.

'Look, I don't have all day. Do you want me to transfer it to DVD or not? I have customers waiting.'

Sweat sticks to my inner T-shirt. I think for a few seconds before answering. 'Just give me a couple of minutes.'

He sighs and moves his attention to the couple that has just entered the shop.

What's behind that song? Is it a favourite wedding song? 'Girl, You'll Be a Woman Soon.' I can't let him transfer the videotape onto a DVD without knowing what's on it. It's my responsibility. Should I ask Dad? That would be a waste of time. Depending on the day, he would give me a different explanation. What if I return the tape to the nursing home and avoid the prob-lem? It's not my tape. But then I'd never know what's behind the song.

I don't have to make it so complicated – the shop assistant transfers the tape to DVD and then I return it to the nursing home. But what if they ask me questions? What do I say? That I took the tape from a box where my father collects stolen items? Or do I simply say that the tape was already transferred to DVD when I found it in the box?

Inside me, the desire to do the right thing or do the unthinkable fight tooth and nail.

I put my legs together and tighten my body. It is

rigid. My right thigh is shaking slightly. Curiosity envelops me like a spider's web. I have to make a decision. I have two options: return the tape to the nursing home or transfer it to DVD.

On the left, the child is now with his mother, who's putting her daughter back in the pushchair. The couple is two metres away from me, talking to the shop assistant. They want some batteries. The shop assistant turns around and opens a drawer, looking for the batteries.

Do I return the tape or convert it to DVD?

Sergeant Jones has advised me to accept the situation as it is. And what does Sergeant Jones know about my situation? What does he know about what I'm going through? The image of Tom with another woman turns my stomach and rage showers my body with adrenaline. Have I been living in a parallel universe? Or a universe for idiots? I don't need to be taught what's right and what's wrong.

My eyes fly from one side of the shop to the other then turn sharply towards the door. I take the camera, turn and walk quickly through the door. The grey of the dusk confuses me for a moment. I walk fast but I don't know which way to go.

Someone shouts my name.

'Megan!'

I increase my pace.

'Megan, Megan!'

It's Margie, my neighbour.

I hold the camera tightly and start to run. The wires are like whips hitting my thighs with every step. My breath comes faster and my heart swells in my chest. Shame doesn't let me stop to witness my own actions.

Margie shouts my name in the distance for the last time.

I'm going crazy.

I keep running until I reach the cemetery.

20

Wednesday, 11 January 2006
Time: 3.21 p.m.

At the cemetery, I push the metal gate but it doesn't give way. I take the knob firmly and squeeze harder. It's rusty and rough to the touch. I struggle uselessly and the palm of my hand gets stained with blood-red rust smelling of mould. An uncontrollable rage makes me feel stronger and I grit my teeth and kick the gate, which squeaks like an old man's moan. It flies open and hits the fence.

Isn't sadness supposed to be the first emotion you feel when you enter a cemetery?

The green of the grass is darker at this time of the afternoon and contrasts with the sombre tones of the tombstones placed in a disorderly way like a game of dominoes.

I follow the path to one of the gravestones, the whitest in the cemetery. The years and the weather have not yet caused it to deteriorate. I bow my head and whisper to it.

'Hi, Amy. I saw your husband this morning. He was on his way to see you. Look what beautiful flowers he brought you.'

I touch the petals with my fingertips. Red roses. Amy's favourites. I bring my nose closer and take a deep breath, but they don't smell of anything.

I sit on a wooden bench and take out a handkerchief to dry my forehead. My breathing is normalising. I fix my eyes on the tombstone. How many times has Oliver come here to cry for Amy? How many times has he crawled to this grave, hugging the tombstone while sobbing with trembling lips over the absence of his wife?

'Look at your majestic tombstone. Your father spared no expense.'

A chill reminds me that my T-shirt is still damp. Amy's angelic face emerges in my memory. So beautiful and full of life.

'You know that I'll soon be thirty-seven, but you, on the other hand, will always be young in everyone's memory.'

I throw my head back and see the same overcast sky as this morning.

'Today my curiosity was stronger than my shame and suddenly I remembered you.' I put my bag aside, which is heavy with the camera in it. 'I've had two pieces of bad news recently: Uncle Paddy has died, and the gynaecologist has told me that I may not be able to have children.' I keep silent as if waiting for an answer that never comes, then continue. 'I've been reflecting. And I think I've made a mistake, although I don't know exactly what. It wasn't the right decision. But I don't know what the wrong decision was. I don't know if you understand me, dear Amy. It's like a state of apathy for the things around me. Well, that and Tom. Would you forgive him?'

My smile tastes like sour milk. Some magpies have landed and are moving nervously through the grass looking for something. I cross my arms, close my fists and my nails press into my palms. I wince. My hand smells of blood. It's the rust from the fence.

'I'm telling you this because I know you won't tell anyone.' I swallow and exhale very slowly. 'I've come to the conclusion that the lives of others, of my neighbours and my friends, seem better to me. It's like their house is bigger, their work is better and their family life is fuller. It's the desire for that sweetie that tastes better in the mouths of others. Maybe that's why Tom looked away from home and gave in to temptation.'

The magpies take flight and leave. I uncross my arms and my fingers play with each other nervously.

'The people I know have nicer houses than mine, have more money, more free time, travel more and love their wives and husbands with the same passion as in the early years. But I guess that, if they look at each other, they have the same feeling I do. They must look at me thinking I've got more time to take care of myself, while they spend hours taking care of their children. It's envy, and I'm the first one to raise my hand. We desire the lives of others. We love the life of others more than our own. And that desire is like an infidelity to ourselves.

This feeling grows inside me and becomes more alive every day. Sometimes it worries me. Other times I don't care.'

A gust of cold air hits my face. Could it be Amy's spirit? It sneaks inside me, brushes my legs and arms, wraps me up and gets its own way. My gaze sinks into Amy's tombstone and a tear blurs my vision.

'Let me tell you a story, my dear Amy. One of my closest friends met a handsome and good man. He had a good job, and he adored my friend. Her dream was to move to a house in the south near the sea, and that dream came true. She dreamed of having a child, and that dream came true too. Her life was one of unusual perfection. She was good and confident. I never heard her husband raise his voice to her or neglect his child. She was Queen Midas. What she touched, turned to gold for her. One day she made a play for Tom. Fortunately for her and unfortunately for me, that dream was also fulfilled; however, it was the beginning of my nightmare.'

My mouth fills with saliva and I swallow in anger. My voice rises and my words escape like ignited gunpowder.

'It happened over six months ago. When I discovered the phone number on Tom's mobile, with a few obvious messages, that was the moment I lost everything.' I move my stiff neck and try to relax my back. 'But you're no longer here, although I feel your presence more than ever.'

I get up and relish every syllable of my words.

'You fucked up, Amy, you fucked up so badly.'

Do I only feel anger when I enter this cemetery?

I turn around and leave the cemetery before I catch pneumonia. I have three missed calls from Sophie and a message from Tom that says, "We need to talk. Kisses."

I don't reply.

I'm going to bury my uncle, return the camera and get it over with.

21

Wednesday, 11 January 2006
Time: 6.16 p.m.

I NEED to hurry up and change my clothes and run, or I'll be late for dinner at Sophie's. I open the wardrobe, take out a pair of clean jeans and put them on with my sky-blue turtleneck jumper. Then I sit on the bed and pull on a pair of knee-high leather boots. I leave the camera on the bedside table next to the teardrop-shaped lamp. The reflection of the light bathes the camera and creates flashes. I run my index finger carefully over its surface, as if it were a coveted treasure.

My cheeks are itching with the same intensity as my curiosity. When I was a child, I used to steal homemade biscuits my mother made for our guests. That was many years ago and I wasn't so aware of my actions. Am I now? I scratch my cheek and pick up my mobile. I pass it from one hand to the other with hesitation while I keep looking at my little treasure. I have a plan.

I leave a voice message for my friend.

'Sophie, I have a terrible headache. I'm staying home tonight. Tomorrow I'll stop by the shop and we'll talk. Thanks for everything today. Kisses.'

I turn off my mobile phone and take the camera in both hands. I swallow and my heart races. Tomorrow I will return the camera. Tomorrow I will return the tape to the nursing home. Tomorrow I will apologise to everyone. I will do all that tomorrow, but today … today the camera is mine.

The doorbell rings. I jump up from the bed and stand as still as a metal bar. It rings again. I'm not expecting anyone. I look out of the window and see Sophie, who raises her head and signals to me to open the door. In one hand she's holding a bag and in the other she's carrying a pizza. She didn't get my message. I go down the stairs, disappointed, and open the door.

'Weren't we going to have dinner at your place?'

She looks at me sheepishly. 'I'm sorry, honey. I forgot it's poker night at home. What do you think? Four men and a desperate woman.' She smiles. 'So I thought I'd better come to yours instead.' She holds up the bag and the pizza to make her decision more obvious.

'Come on in.'

'I brought your favourite, pepperoni pizza. By the way, the Italian guy we like has left. And here is some wine and chocolate ice cream to help to digest the pizza. What do you think?' She winks at me.

'You read my mind.'

She sits at the kitchen table, pleased. 'Put the pizza

in the oven for a few minutes. Look, this just came out,' she says, holding up a magazine.

'What is it this time? Another wedding magazine?'

She ignores my comment. 'I'm going to read you something.'

'The horoscope?' I reply with irony.

'No, Mrs Sceptic. Something better.'

I sit opposite her with my elbows on the table, and the smell of pizza opens a hole in my stomach. I'm not eating much these days. Shall I tell her about the camera? She opens the wine and pours me a glass.

'You know what, Sophie?' I lean back and shrug my shoulders. 'I have a stupid feeling that my uncle ran away that night, and that caused his death.'

'Ran away where?' She takes a sip of wine.

'I don't know where. But he ran away from something.' I shrug my shoulders even more and say it out loud. 'Something that killed him.'

Sophie's smile fades from her face. I look away from my sister's painting and my voice becomes listless. 'I'm sorry. I don't think I'm explaining this well.'

'I understand you, honey.'

'Well…'

She takes my hand. 'I'm serious.' And she gives me a smile.

'Do you believe me? Because I also did something stupid today.'

'Of course I believe you. When my mother died, I had the same feeling. She spent days insisting on going to the hospital and I thought it was one of her many performances to get attention. Once there…' She sighs, looking at nothing. 'Well, you know. She died.'

I move my head slightly. Sophie doesn't understand me either.

The beep of the oven warns us that the pizza is ready. I get up and set the table.

'And what stupid thing did you do today? You can't break a plate even if you try to.'

'You're not going to put away that magazine?'

'No, look, let's play a game.'

'A game?' I bite into the pizza and the cheese burns me. I take a quick sip of wine and dry my lips.

Sophie turns pages of the magazine with one hand, while feeding herself a slice of pizza with the other.

'Here.' She lifts the magazine to show me a page and says loudly, 'Know yourself and be happier. You need pen and paper.'

'Sophie, you're like a dog with a bone.' I pick out a pen and a notebook from the drawer and pass them to her.

'No, I'm not doing it. It's personal. You write it.'

'Write what?'

'Write down, number one.' She takes another sip of wine, puts down her slice of pizza and continues with a ceremonial tone. 'Let's imagine you're walking in a forest.'

'Do I have to close my eyes?'

'No. You have to write.'

'A forest?'

She nods. I lean forward, fidget with the pen and let

my imagination run wild. 'A forest of small firs lined up symmetrically.'

'Write it down, but don't tell me. Second question. Is it day or night?'

I think for a moment. 'It's neither day nor night. Something in between. Dawn or dusk.'

'Write it down. Don't tell me. Now, for the third question, you need to describe the path.'

'A path?' I put my pen to my lip while trying to imagine a path in my forest. 'There is no path.'

'There has to be a path.'

'Not in my forest.'

'Up to you, you need to go through it. The forest represents the kind of person you are, and the path is your life path. So, you must have a path.'

Am I a forest of small firs lined up symmetrically? Am I so square? Is there no path in my life? I finish my wine and pour another one.

'Well, we're not doing well. How many questions are there?' My voice is full of irony, and I laugh. When was the last time I had a good time in my life?

'Let me see.' Sophie runs her index finger over the page. 'Twelve in total.'

'Can I please have a summary? Chocolate ice cream?'

'When you don't feel like it…' And she nods to my proposal. 'Write down, you find a pot, a bear and a house.'

I get up and serve two bowls of ice cream. 'But can't I tell you?'

'No, it's personal.' She shakes her head.

I scribble a few notes. A big, ugly bear. I dodge it while catching a pot of gold. I run and reach a wooden hut. I enter and lock it. 'Done.' I raise the notebook to Sophie and show her the answers. A big, ugly bear, an old gold pot and a wooden hut.

She raises her hand and covers my notes. 'It's personal. It's for you. The bear is directly proportional to the way you perceive your problems, the pot represents your connection to your ancestors, the hut is your dreams and prosperity. And here is the penultimate one.'

'I think we're done. I also think I failed because I didn't answer the questions correctly. The hut is falling apart.'

Sophie ignores my comment and continues reading. 'A man knocks on the door and asks you to open it.'

'Not in my wildest dreams.' I serve the ice cream.

'Shh! Don't tell me. Write it down. This represents the degree of trust you have in people.'

I leave the spoon in the bowl. Is that true? My intuition doesn't let me trust Tom. Neither did the police convince me, and I found Father Jonathan's attitude strange... Have I become so cynical? I don't feel like laughing any more.

'And here's the last question.' Sophie raises the magazine and stretches every word with a halo of mystery.

Then her mobile phone rings suddenly and the magic disappears.

'Hi, love. Yes. I'm sorry, I didn't realise the time. I'm leaving soon. No, I don't want you to drive. I'm sure you've been drinking with your friends. I'll take the bus. I'll text you when I'm on my way.' She hangs up and looks at me with her innocent, sheepish smile, and before she says anything, I reassure her.

'Nothing to say. Paul is waiting for you at home and I need to sleep.'

I don't like Paul either, to be honest.

Sophie gets up, gives me a hug and whispers in my ear, 'Would you like to be my bridesmaid?'

I feel her tenderness piercing my bones. 'I would love to.' I hope she's right this time. She deserves a good man by her side. 'You're leaving me hanging. What's the last question?'

'Oh, yes.' She takes the magazine. 'Let me see. This is the representation of death or the lack of changes in life. Here it says, "Suddenly everything disappears, the house, the man, the forest, and you don't know where you are. No matter how much you shout, no one can hear you or help you.''

My legs are shaking and, although I'm breathing, there is no oxygen in my lungs. Sophie is concentrating on reading. I hold on to the kitchen table. There's something I've experienced, but I cannot locate it in a specific place or time. The more I dig into my mind, the darker everything becomes. I tense my fingers and scratch the surface. I only remember the emotion. A basic emotion, an intense emotion, a deep emotion: restlessness, agitation, disturbance. Panic in its purest form.

Sophie continues, 'What do you do? Do you give up? Do you fight?'

The pen is still in my hand and, as if a spirit from

the past has possessed me and controlled my arm, I scribble my answer: I run.

22

Wednesday, 11 January 2006
Time: 10.11 p.m.

I HAVE a bath with menthol salts, put on my pink plush dressing gown and lie in bed. The video camera is on the bedside table. I take it and feel it with my hands to confirm that it's real and not the product of my imagination. Yesterday I lied and today I stole. I don't know what sin I will commit tomorrow.

I plug in the headphones, turn off the teardrop-shaped lamp and leave the camera on my chest. I lift the tab off the small screen with my fingernail, press the play button and focus on the ceiling. The smell of menthol envelops the room in the gloom. The light of the screen covers my face. I tense my legs and arch my back. Several vertebrae crack. The stiffness has almost disappeared from my legs. I close my eyes and let myself be carried away by Neil Diamond's hoarse voice singing his "Girl, You'll Be a Woman Soon".

I miss going out with my friends. The laughs, the jokes and the last-minute gossip. Since I left the hospital, I have lost the desire to see them. Isabel moved to Cambridge with a lawyer from a wealthy family. Paula is too busy with her two children, the dog and her in-laws. The only one left is Maryam, my colleague and now a supervisor. She went on maternity leave a couple of weeks ago and is now living with her parents in Wales for the next few months before giving birth. The child is not her husband's, but he doesn't know that.

The song ends and I wake up from my thoughts. The tape continues. A silence interrupted by some background noises that are mixed with a woman's laugh. I get up slowly and rest my back against the headboard. I think I can hear a slight grunt from a child too. It must be a home video of a special event. A wedding? Yes, maybe it's a wedding. That would explain the background music. Or maybe a party? But I don't hear people. Besides, it's too short. A trip, maybe?

This summer Tom insisted we take a trip to the Canary Islands. On the way back, when we landed, he got a call from the newspaper. He took a taxi to the newsroom; I took a taxi home. I got angry. On the way home I realised that our life had become boring, and with it came the worst cancer in a relationship: routine.

I take a deep breath and my lungs are impregnated with menthol. I expel the air and a bitter taste remains in my mouth.

I open my eyes. The room is still dark. I rewind to the beginning. There's something buried in this tape that I'm going to dig up tonight. I blink several times to get my eyes used to the light on the screen. Several minutes go by, but the tape is empty. My eyes start to get irritated and become watery. I blink again and a tear runs down my cheek. I lift my head and look out the window. The light from the street passes through the glass and creates shadows inside the room. The music plays again, but my eyes are still suspended, looking at the shadows in the room. I don't dare look at the screen. I'm wary. Perhaps afraid?

The song ends and I hear that woman's laugh and child's grunt again. I turn up the volume. Now I think it sounds more like a groan. My gaze is frozen in nothingness. The groaning goes on for a few seconds and increases and then suddenly stops. Should I look? I press stop and switch on the lamp.

I stand up and walk from left to right, then stop. I haven't come this far not to know what's on this damn tape.

I rewind the tape for the third time. I press play, harder, and look at the screen as if my life were at stake. The battery is half full. After a few seconds the colony of grey ants moves nervously on the screen. I run my hand through my hair without taking my eyes off the screen and approach the small window. Without looking away, I pull the curtains closed. I squeeze my hand on the fabric to make sure they're drawn. Nobody sees me. I move my toes. I hold the camera with both hands as if it's a stone weighing a hundredweight. The knot in my dressing gown is undone and I'm only wearing a pair of knickers underneath.

The minutes before the song take forever, and my

body has an adrenaline rush. My heart beats fast and my breathing is more rapid. I breathe through my mouth as if breathing through my nose isn't enough. A tingle runs through my arms to my fingertips. As I hold the camera, I search and touch my fingertips together. They are cold.

The seconds are ticking, and I breathe deeply. I open my mouth more and, with each breath, my heart tries to catch up with my breathing. I feel like I'm drowning. I'm hyperventilating. As if my body is warning me of an unseen danger.

I don't give up. The dark light radiates from the screen and attracts me like a siren's song. I pause a little to regulate my breathing and take a deep, slow breath. The pauses are longer. Seconds later I hold my breath as if I am underwater and count to ten. My heartbeat slows down until it reaches a normal rhythm. An uncontrollable desire keeps me looking at the screen, watching that small window and contemplating the situation. Then the image begins to move. It is a dark room.

I take off my headphones and leave the camera lying on the bed. I haven't stopped it and it continues. I move my legs and arms as if checking that my soul is still inside my body. My hands are no longer cold. Sweat runs down my forehead. How convenient, I say to myself. Another hot flush.

I bite my lower lip. I'm invading someone's private life. Someone I don't know. Or maybe I do? I don't know yet. I feel for the headphones and plug them into my ears again. I turn up the volume even more and the *shh* sound is more intense. After seven seconds in a darkened room, a silhouette materialises. The silhouette of a woman.

I bring my face closer as if I were sneaking into that little window. On a fixed plane, the small silhouette wiggles to the sound of music. I move the screen slightly as if I could focus more closely. As if it were a 3D image that I could get closer to and see the edges. The drums, the guitar and the voice rumble in my ears. Who is this woman?

She slowly shakes out her long straight hair, and it covers her face. The dark colour of her hair blends in with the gloom of the room and makes it difficult to distinguish her face. She's wearing a light shirt, I would say white, and a dark skirt, dark green perhaps, with checks. She seems to be looking at me. Intensely. As real as if she were going to jump off the screen, as if she were here in my room dancing. Do I know this woman?

The mysterious woman lifts her arms to the sound of Neil Diamond's voice and starts to unbutton her shirt. I frown. She loses another button. And then another one and another one, until a line of white flesh forms from her neck to her navel, contrasting with the shadows of the room.

I stop the tape and go into the bathroom to think. Okay. I know what it is. A woman doing a striptease. Who? I swallow a couple of aspirin with a big shot of water and leave the glass on the sink. I don't care about the woman and who she's stripping for. It's private. I lie down on the bed again, and a question arises: do I want to return the tape to the nursing home now?

I close my eyes and wait for tomorrow. But

tomorrow doesn't come. I make a mental list of things I have to do this week and conclude that I should put speculation aside and concentrate on my poor Uncle Paddy's funeral, but my head spins as I lie in bed.

I turn on the lamp and look at the ceiling of my room. A greyish blue. I stand up again. Embarrassment catches me, but my curiosity wins out and I press play again. I study the woman's movements as she unbuttons her shirt. I've never seen her before.

She looks at a lover, possibly a husband or a partner. Then she drops her shirt and shows herself naked to me, white flesh in the shadows. Dad keeps objects to not forget the people he loves. Who does Dad not want to forget? I stop the video. Then I close my eyes and wait for tomorrow.

23

Thursday, 12 January 2006
Time: 6.31 a.m.

I WAKE up suddenly with the image of the mysterious woman dancing in my head. Who could she be? A nurse from my father's nursing home? Someone from the area? Does it matter? The tape isn't mine. Shouldn't I focus on my uncle's funeral?

It is now dawn outside, although the street retains the grey cold of winter. I could do with some fresh air before handing the camera over to its owner, apologising a thousand times and returning the tape to Dad's memory box.

I put on black leggings and a sports bra, then a dark-blue polyester T-shirt with a lightweight jacket that protects from the cold air. This time, my cotton socks are thicker, and I'm going to try out my new green trainers that match the jacket.

I review on the board the distances run in the last

few days and the goal I have for today. I've reached almost ten and a half miles. About ninety minutes, forty-five each way.

I go downstairs to the kitchen and have a coffee on an empty stomach before going out for my run. On the street, the wind is blowing hard and it feels colder than it is. The winter here is very treacherous, since the humidity level rises as you get closer to the coast. I increase my pace and start to warm up. Running on grass gives better cushioning than running on tarmac and reduces the risk of injury. I go up and down small hills, and the image of the woman dancing persists in my head. What would motivate a woman to let herself be recorded on video doing a striptease? Money? Her love for the man? Are we stupid?

Some studies written by men confirm that it's more difficult for women to break their own records than for men. This is due to hormone levels. Hormones and men, always side by side. You can find all kinds of men, although Tom has never asked me to perform a strip-tease on camera. I'd have died of shame. It doesn't matter any more, anyway.

An idea pops into my head. A little suspicion. I hope I'm wrong, but I'll have to watch the video one last time.

I increase my speed, but my knees suffer. When I had problems in the past, I used pads to keep my knees more supported, but they didn't make it easy for me to move around, so I stopped using them and contacted a specialist, who taught me some techniques to avoid putting weight on my knees or injuring my back. Long steps can damage the vertebrae of the spine as they work harder to cushion the impact of running.

I'm approaching a downhill slope. I try to slow down so as not to overload my knees. My breathing rhythm is stable, and my heart rate is also within a range of 150 to 155. Now I continue along a straight line. In the distance I see a group of scattered cows grazing. Free of worries.

Soon I've gone beyond five and a half miles and I'm saying goodbye to the cows and the bucolic picture. I'm going home. I keep running, maintaining the same heart rate. My feet are wet from the dew of the grass and my forehead from sweat.

An hour and a half after setting out, I return home. My brain is bathed in serotonin, and in the centre of my mind a doubt in the form of a woman dances and spins. I only hope that my suspicions aren't right.

The more I run, the more time I have to spend stretching to avoid injury. Otherwise the muscles stiffen and hurt afterwards, as they did on Sunday.

I enter the house, take a shower and proudly write another eleven miles on the board. I've run the longest distance of my life, eleven miles, and have no one to congratulate me.

Then I go downstairs to the kitchen and make myself some eggs on slightly hard rye toast. The fridge is empty. There are only a couple of green apples left in the fruit bowl.

I rewind the tape and put the camera on the table next to my plate with the eggs on toast. The tape lasts fifteen minutes: eleven minutes are blank and four minutes with the mysterious woman performing a striptease. I start eating. Minutes later I hear the music and see the woman. She moves her straight black hair, but I still can't make out her face. Everything is dark, full of shadows. I put my fork and knife down without looking away from the screen. Why would anyone want to participate in the recording of such a dance, if you can hardly see?

She takes off her skirt while she's still dancing. The shirt barely covers her thighs. Her hair dances with her. She's a small young woman.

Does it make me sick to see this video?

No, I'm not like that. I take a napkin. The right word is empathy, a strange bond of empathy with that mysterious woman.

The last button on the shirt is unbuttoned. It's the last minute of the song. I swallow a bite of eggs on toast. I don't have any juice left. Suddenly the answer jumps out. Now I understand. It's obvious. The woman is looking at the man in front of her, not at the camera lens. I squeeze the napkin tightly. She doesn't know she's being recorded. It's a hidden video.

I've lost my appetite. I put the napkin on the plate, then throw the remainder of my breakfast in the bin. I take an apple from the fruit bowl and bite it hard.

My father has to explain to me where he got the video.

24

Thursday, 12 January 2006
Time: 8.19 a.m.

I APPROACH THE RECEPTION DESK, but no one comes to meet me. The floor is wet and smells of bleach. A small woman is mopping the corridor. She moves her head, absorbed by the rhythm of the music in her head-phones. Is she the woman from the video? I call her, but she doesn't answer. Will I now wonder if every small woman I see is the one from the video? I walk towards her, being careful not to leave any footprints on the floor.

'Don't you see it's wet?' she says, grumpily.

'There's no one at the reception desk.'

'I'm just the cleaner. Ask one of the nurses. Over there.' And she points down the hall in the opposite direction.

I stand still. I check that the videotape is still in my bag and take out some mints.

'Don't wait for the floor to dry, I'll give it another wash.' The cleaner adjusts her headphones and continues with her task.

There is no nurse to ask, so I continue down the corridor to my father's room.

Will he remember our conversation yesterday, and perhaps not remember the absence of Uncle Paddy? He doesn't even ask about Katherine any more.

I knock on his door. 'Dad, it's Megan.'

No answer. Maybe he's having breakfast in the dining room. A key hangs from the doorknob and an empty laundry basket labelled *Mr Hudson* is waiting patiently by the door frame. I knock again.

'Dad?'

Mum always said that it was rude to show up unannounced, and that it was an invasion of privacy to open letters that weren't yours. Katherine stopped talking to me for almost a year because I opened one of her letters. That was when she was sneaking around with that boy from public school. We had the same last name, and I thought the letter was for me. Well, maybe I wanted to believe that. Besides, the envelope was already open.

I push the laundry basket aside and open the door slowly.

'Dad, I'm coming in. Are you there?'

A hospital bed covered with messy sheets sits by closed windows covered by double-lined curtains. On the other side of the small room, a slim, low-lustre wardrobe stands next to the bathroom door. In the corner, between the windows and the bed, there is a bedside table with a cluttered collection of practical objects: a handheld lamp, a telephone, a plastic cup with water, a radio and a clock. There are no photos or flowers.

'Dad, you need to get more organised.' But I'm talking to the walls.

Dad's practicality has evaporated over time. I draw the curtains, open the windows and put the sheets in the laundry basket.

Someone flushes the toilet. My neck tightens. Am I in the wrong room?

'Dad?' I ask, clenching my teeth.

Noises come from behind the bathroom door. I take a crablike step backwards in the direction of the main corridor. It's too late. The bathroom door opens.

'You're late again.' He has an authoritative expression and walks towards me as if looking for the straight line between us.

'I'm sorry, Dad, I've been busy and couldn't come to see you earlier.' I take the videotape out of my bag and show it to him. 'Have you seen this tape before?'

'No. What day is it today?'

'Thursday. This tape was in your memory box. Is it from a nurse? Someone here? Do you remember?'

'Thursday…' he repeats with hesitation.

I force a smile. He's not having a good day.

I open the wardrobe door. Several shirts and a jacket are hanging there. The drawers are arranged as I left them last time. Below are the shoes that I gave him as a present, made to measure with more space on the sides for his bunions. Under the shirts and above the shoebox, a miniature boat is anchored.

'Is that the boat Uncle Paddy gave you? I found this tape in your memory box. Do you know whose it is?' I ask.

'It's not a boat,' he replies with a dry tone, and grabs the model. 'It's an oil tanker.'

'Do you need to bring it with you to breakfast? Do you want to keep the tape in your memory box? Can I label it with the name of the person so that you remember?'

He taps the ground with his foot and rubs his face.

My forced smile relaxes and feels more authentic. I come closer and give him a hug. Dad used to go away for long periods of time, working for an American oil company, and Uncle Paddy would help take care of us. Every year, he would take Katherine and me to Catholic Action Summer Camp, although Katherine didn't like all that sharing, singing and praying. One night she ran away, and when Dad found out about it, he slapped her. Mum started crying. Uncle Paddy scolded Dad and comforted Mum.

'It's an oil tanker. Look, this is the davit, here's the rudder and the propeller. Behind the propeller is the engine room...'

'But, Dad, you don't need to take this boat to breakfast. It might get broken.'

'It's not a boat.'

'I know. It's an oil tanker. Uncle Paddy gave you this model and helped you build it. It's beautiful. Maybe it's better if it stays in your room.'

'People here mistake a merchant ship for an oil tanker. They need to know where I work. I work on an oil tanker.' He points his finger and continues, 'Here, above, is the cargo transfer area. See? And below, here, is the tank.'

'It's okay, Dad.' I sigh. 'Bring it to the dining room.'

He shuffles out the door with the toy in his hands. I rub my eyes. I'm tired. The black nurse from the other day is by the door with a trolley, watching us.

'Good morning. I've come to see my father,' I explain before being asked.

'Don't bother. I'm not curious. I came to pick up the dirty bedding.' She pauses, and looks at me like a child about to let a secret slip out. 'You might have seen the shoebox?'

'What about it?'

She comes up to me. 'You should know this.' She whispers, 'Your father hides useless things under his mattress like a magpie. I wondered why an old man would hide useless things under his bed, as if they were money.' She opens her eyes wider, obviously hoping I'll agree with her. 'I got tired of it,' she continues in a theatrical tone, 'and took them all away. I was going to throw them in the bin. But of course, in this nursing home I have to ask permission even to go to the bathroom.' She lets go of the trolley and put her hands together. 'So, I asked the head nurse, and the doctor came and said no, I wasn't allowed to throw anything away. I had to keep the objects because they help him to keep his mind afloat. They're memories. Like that boat … well, oil tan-ker,' she says, stressing every syllable with a slight edge to her voice. 'So I put them in a shoebox in the wardrobe.'

'Have you seen this tape?'

She takes it from me without asking.

'This relic?' She snorts and gives it back to me. 'No. People record with mobile phones these days.'

'What's that doctor's name?'

'Who?'

'The doctor you mentioned.'

'Oh, Dr Johnson. He was the one who interviewed me.'

I keep my distance. 'By the way, his name is Anthony.'

'No, no. His name is Dr Johnson.'

I hold my bag tightly and repeat, 'My father's name is Anthony. He's not a magpie.'

Her eyes open dramatically. 'Oh, no. I didn't mean that—'

'Is the doctor around? Can I see him?'

She nods. 'Follow me.'

Maybe the doctor will give me the clue I'm looking for.

25

Thursday, 12 January 2006
Time: 8.46 a.m.

We stop by one of the residents' rooms. Music floats out from inside. It is the voice of a black woman dressed in jazz, rescued from a book by Scott Fitzgerald.

'Stay here, please. I'm going to ask the head nurse,' the nurse says as she parks her trolley.

I'm curious to know about the music that emanates from the room. Inside, a tall, thin woman is making the bed, her back to the door while the other nurse whispers in her ear. The head nurse doesn't look like the woman in the video either.

An old woman sits and sways in a rocking chair, absorbed by the music. Her hair is like snow that falls and swings on her fragile shoulders. She holds her hands together in her lap. We look at each other for a few seconds. My cheeks are blushing, but between her wrinkles, there is a smile on her thin lips.

'Would you like to dance?' she asks affectionately.

'Sorry?'

The two nurses turn around suddenly.

'What are you doing here?' asks the head nurse, in a Slavic accent.

'I'm sorry. I'd like to see Dr Johnson.'

'That's what my colleague was telling me. What are you doing here?' she repeats.

The natural light that comes through the window reflects on her white skin, and her inquisitive pale blue eyes look at me with disapproval.

I take a clumsy step backwards. 'I'm sorry.'

She comes closer. 'I am Irenka Kramarski, head nurse in charge. We are short-staffed today: one nurse is sick and two are on maternity leave. Have you signed the register?'

The black nurse hides a smile. She takes her trolley and continues on her way.

'Yes, I signed the register.'

The old lady swings her hand in the air and says to me, 'See you soon. Very soon.'

The tendons in my legs tighten and I bite my lower lip. The head nurse ushers me out then closes the door and follows me down the corridor.

'You don't need to worry about your father. He's being well taken care of. If you want, you can have breakfast with him while my colleague tidies up his room.'

'That sounds perfect. I'd just like to see Dr Johnson.'

'The doctor is in his consultation room, at the end of the corridor.'

'Thank you.'

'Be careful not to go into the wrong room. As they say in your language, curiosity killed the cat.'

I look down. 'I'll knock before I go in.'

I go down the narrow corridor and turn left. Someone has left a tap running and it still smells of cleaning products.

I knock on the door cautiously.

'Come in.'

I go in slowly and find a young-looking man in a white doctor's coat. He has white brushstrokes in the hair at his temples and is wearing a pair of rimless glasses.

'Dr Johnson, I'm Mr Hudson's daughter. If you have a minute, I'd like to talk to you.'

'Sure.' He raises his hand in an invitation to sit down.

The visitor's chair is made of dark brown leather identical to the doctor's chair and the room is a clinical white.

'What can I do for you?'

'Doctor, I'd like to know who visits my father.'

His eyebrows twitch. 'Are you not happy with the care we give to your father here in the nursing home? We're making changes to the staff—'

'It's not that.'

'So, what is it?'

I look down, taking a moment to make up an excuse. On the table is a picture of Dr Johnson and his wife in the country with bikes and backpacks. They're both smiling. The woman has Asian features and her hair is cut in a very short bob.

'Mrs Evans?'

'Does your wife work as a doctor?'

If the videotape was left in this nursing home, the woman in the video cannot be very far away. But what do I do if I find her? Do I tell her that I have a video of her performing a striptease, and that it was recorded without her consent? That my father stole the videotape from somewhere and kept it in his collection of personal objects?

The doctor looks at the picture and glows with pride.

'No. She's a secondary school teacher,' he replies, adjusting the angle of the photo in his direction.

'Oh, like Oliver,' I say without thinking. "And does your wife visit you a lot here?'

He looks at me with bewilderment and I want to eat my words.

'Mrs Evans, I don't understand the nature of your visit. I would appreciate it if you could be more specific.'

I'm trying to get around the conversation.

'Don't get me wrong. I'm happy with the care my father receives, but I think he's had visits from someone, and I'd like to know who it is.'

The doctor listens with interest, running his index finger over the photo frame. When I finish, he takes a few seconds before answering. He raises his eyes and fixes them on mine.

'What makes you think so?'

'The box of objects he has.'

'I recommended to the head nurse that your father keep the items in a box. It's a way to keep his memory afloat.'

'I saw it. I think it's good he keeps things. Anything that will help him keep his memory afloat, as you say, but I want to know who's visiting him.'

The doctor looks at his watch and adjusts his wedding ring. 'According to our policy, residents only receive visits from their closest relatives. And if other people would like to come, we consult the relatives first. In this case, you.' His voice becomes more distant, as if he were reading aloud from a book. 'Have you not been informed of the policy?'

'I'm aware of the policy, and I know there is an entry register.'

'Of course. Do you question the safety of our residents?'

His gesture is somewhat melodramatic.

'Not at all. I'm sorry. I didn't mean to be rude. I didn't think it would be a problem to allow a direct relative access to information about a resident's visitors.'

'What makes you think that your father has received unusual visits?'

I've been caught. 'I don't know.'

I play with my bag, put my hand inside and feel the videotape. Did my father steal it? Maybe it was given to him. But what for?

'I just would be more reassured if I could take a look.'

'If I show you the register, it would violate the privacy of our residents. Only the authorities would be allowed. You understand me? Only for a compelling reason, such as a police investigation.'

'I understand.' I swallow, and nod several times.

Ground, swallow me up.

Someone knocks on the door. The doctor ignores it and stares at me. 'Mrs Evans, do you have a compelling reason?'

I take my hand out of my bag. 'Not at all,' I answer emphatically.

'Then you have to trust our professionalism. Come in!'

'I'll go now.'

A nurse comes in and I walk out the door with my head down.

Have I been brave by daring to play Sherlock Holmes? Or a coward for not telling him the truth?

It's easier in the movies.

I have another option. Although it's a little riskier.

26

Thursday, 12 January 2006
Time: 9.06 a.m.

I GO into the dining room and look for Dad. That gives me an excuse to stay a little longer and try another option to find out who visited him.

I move aside to let some old people into the room. Others are having breakfast alone or with the help of the nurses. Three women are crocheting and a man is standing by the window alone. He holds a pocket watch in his hand, daydreaming. Perhaps with people he no longer sees.

Dad is arguing with the nurse.

'I don't want this tray,' he grumbles. 'I want that one.'

'They're the same. Porridge, fruit, toast, unsalted butter,' the nurse replies in a bored tone.

'I said that one there.' And he points to the tray at the bottom of the trolley.

'As you wish. Here you are, Mr Hudson.'

He's sitting at the back of the dining room, in a corner by the window. As he places the boat carefully on the chair next to him, his hand is shaking.

I walk slowly towards him.

To start with, he began forgetting small details of everyday life: losing the car keys, getting disoriented when leaving the supermarket, or keeping his wallet in the fridge. One day, Margie found him crying outside my house when I was travelling with Tom. He was lost.

After many tests, the results were clear. Moderate irreversible cognitive impairment – phase two Alzheimer's.

I put my hand on his shoulder.

'Dad, do you want me to get you something to drink?'

'Tea would be nice.'

'Sounds good to me too.'

He grabs my arm, pulls me down and whispers, 'Don't tell him it's for me.'

I nod and play along. The black nurse with the trolley passes by the dining room door with a carefree look. Here's the opportunity I've been waiting for.

'Hi again,' I say with a smile. 'Dr Johnson told me that they're restructuring the staff. I hope it's going to be less stressful.'

The nurse is fidgeting with a cloth and tells me in a boastful tone, 'It's the same stress. Between you and me, this nursing home needs more staff. We can't cope. And every elderly resident is a world of need.'

'I'm so sorry, but I forgot to sign the register earlier.'

She stops fidgeting with the cloth and lifts her chin. 'Didn't you tell the head nurse that you did?'

'Well…' I hesitate. 'I was in a rush and I didn't know what to say. When I saw you, I suddenly remembered.'

'Don't worry.' Her voice is even more dramatic. 'Sometimes people come and go as they please.' She throws the cloth over the trolley. 'Come with me and sign it.'

'Don't worry. You've got work to do. Tell me where it is and I'll sign it on my way out.'

Her expression changes. She crosses her arms and looks me up and down, squinting. Her lips form a circle, and a snort comes out of her mouth. I keep smiling forcibly, tensing my right leg so that she doesn't see I'm hitting the floor with my heel.

'I like you,' she says. 'The new register is behind the reception desk. In the first drawer.'

'May I have permission to go behind the reception desk?'

An uncontrollable laugh with thirty-two white teeth startles me.

'Who? Me? Yes, yes. I give you permission.' She keeps laughing.

I go to the reception desk and look from side to side. There's no one in the corridor. I take the register out of the drawer and hide it inside my coat. I swallow, but my throat is dry. I go straight to the bathroom and lock the door.

The nursing home only has fifteen residents, sometimes even fewer if there's a death. The doctors rotate weekly and I've never seen a woman doctor. There are four men on the nursing staff, two of whom are trainees, and there are six female nurses, as far as I remember – the new head nurse, three assistant nurses and two on maternity leave. One of the assistant nurses is the black woman with the trolley, and there are two slightly older women. Because of their age and complexion, I doubt they would be willing to perform a striptease. That leaves only the two nurses on maternity leave. One is from Pakistan and the other from Equatorial Guinea. Their appearance doesn't fit with the woman in the video. There are also a couple of part-time cleaners, but neither of them would fit either.

I open the register and look for my father's name and the dates of entry. My name appears almost daily, Uncle Paddy only once a week. Tom appears last month and Katherine three months ago. Where the hell would he get the tape? Who did he steal it from? Or did someone give it to him? What's the value of a tape of a woman performing a striptease inside a memory box of an old man with Alzheimer's? I touch Uncle Paddy's signature and give him a kiss. My lower jaw trembles and I swallow again.

Dad is waiting for me with the tea.

I close the register, cover it with my coat and walk quickly to the reception desk and put the register back.

'Are you still here?'

My neck weakens and a little moan escapes me. I don't dare look. It's the disgruntled voice of the head nurse.

'I'm going to have breakfast with my father. He looks sad.'

'From the reception desk?'

I ignore her question and keep walking. I go back to Dad's table with a teapot and two cups. Dad is talking to another swollen-looking man dragging an oxygen bottle.

'This is my daughter Megan,' he introduces me proudly.

'Nice to meet you,' I say as I sit down.

'A very beautiful woman. Your hair matches the colour of your cheeks.' His voice is hoarse and almost inaudible.

'Thank you.'

'Do you have a cigarette?'

'I'm sorry, I don't smoke.'

'Only one daughter?' he asks my father.

'Yes, just one.'

Katherine visited Dad three months ago. Doesn't he remember his own daughter? The man says goodbye and goes on his way. I serve the tea.

'Why didn't you want the tray the nurse offered you?'

'No way,' he says flatly.

'Why?'

'They want to poison me.'

'Dad, no one wants to poison you.'

'Yes, they do.'

I take a deep breath. He's having a bad day. Mine isn't looking too good either. He sits still, considering the bowl with the porridge and the spoon with a perplexed look.

'Dad, it's getting cold.'

He refuses to eat. Why is he so nervous? When I realise why, melancholy envelops me and I feel very lonely next to him.

I take another bowl and spoon for myself. 'Can I have breakfast with you?'

He nods.

He watches how I use the spoon and copies me. He's calmer now. I put the videotape on the table, but he doesn't say anything. I take a sip of tea while watching his movements. He looks at the tape sideways and continues eating.

I finish my tea and leave the cup on the table. I'll try another day. I put on my coat and put the tape back in my bag.

'I'm leaving now, Dad.'

He takes a napkin, wipes his mouth without hurrying and says, looking at the plate, 'I think that tape is from your Uncle Paddy.'

I look at him as if I don't understand. 'What did you just say?'

'When is Paddy coming back?'

I squeeze Dad's shoulder and move it as if to wake him up from a dream.

'Dad, whose videotape is this? Dad, answer me.' And I shake him without thinking about what I'm doing.

My stomach turns as if I had ingested cyanide. He doesn't respond. He's now like a lifeless rag doll with his head down looking at his empty plate. He's without reason.

I sigh deeply, ashamed, and don't look around at anyone as I try to regain my composure.

I have to find the woman in the video, and I think I know how.

27

Thursday, 12 January 2006
Time: 12.19 p.m.

I GO into our garage and rummage in Tom's toolbox. Screws, nails, screwdrivers, a spanner, dry paint cans and cobwebs. My nose is itching from the dust. It's not in here.

I lift several boxes from the shelves. In one box there's an old stained overall, a jar of turpentine and several brushes of different sizes. In the next, a gas cooker with other camping utensils. A snort escapes me. It's been years since we went camping. I open the third box and find an old supermarket bag, with ropes and cables. I take the bag and, when I go out, I hit my right shin on the metal door. I grit my teeth to avoid letting out a whimper.

I limp to the living room, close the curtains and bring the floor lamp next to the TV. I move it so the light focuses on the back of the TV. I empty the bag, and several dozen cables and cords spread out on the floor like snakes.

I didn't have time to take off my coat and the heating is on. I throw my coat on the floor and roll up my sleeves, then get down on my knees. My right shin hurts but my curiosity is stronger than the pain and I have a goal to achieve: to find that woman.

Dad claims that the tape was given to him by Uncle Paddy. And who gave the tape to my uncle? Why did he keep it in my father's memory box? But what if Dad is wrong? His mind is a jumble of incoherent memories. He doesn't even remember his own daughter, Katherine. Maybe he stole the tape from somewhere in the nursing home and the woman in the video is the partner of one of the nurses or doctors. An erotic game between spouses. One of those home videos that are recorded and forgotten in some drawer and, by accident, it ended up in Dad's hands.

But I'm almost certain that the woman doesn't know she's being recorded, since she doesn't look at the camera at any time, while the husband is supposedly behind it. Conclusion: the recording was not made in a consensual manner.

Digging into the skein of cables, I compare the plugs of the TV and the camera. I keep digging until I find the cable I'm looking for. Bingo. For once, I'm glad that Tom has kept all this old stuff. The TV screen is big enough to get a better picture of the mysterious woman.

I connect the plug to the TV set and the camera. The home phone rings several times, but no message is left. Now my mobile rings, but I ignore that too. I get a voice message notification. Who could be looking for me? I'll listen to it later.

I have no time to waste.

I sit in front of the TV on the carpet with my legs crossed in the shape of a lotus flower. I press the play button and a greyish-blue light illuminates the screen. I watch the whole tape from the beginning so that nothing escapes me.

My image is reflected on the screen and the light distorts the features of my face, turning me into a spectre. The little girl from the film *Poltergeist* comes into my mind, and I repeat in a whisper the phrase, 'They're here…'

If it's true that my uncle gave the tape to Dad, assuming that the woman gave the video to Uncle Paddy first, why would a woman who gets naked on video give the tape to the sacristan of the village? Besides, she didn't know she was being recorded. It would have to be someone else who gave the video to my uncle. But who? Why? What did he have to hide?

Neil Diamond's music sounds and a flock of bats push at my stomach to escape. My eyes dive into the screen, and the air in the room seems scarce. The woman in the background appears again like a ghost in the twilight. It's the same movements, the same music, the same halo of mystery. The scene becomes larger, the contours expand and the woman's presence becomes clearer. My fingers run across the glass of the screen, touching the image of the woman and blending in with the image. My world stops.

I will find you.

At first, I thought that the contrast of light and shadow was causing a glint in her hair. That's not it. The hair falls straight and covers a large part of her face. But there's something curious – a white streak down the right side of her black hair.

It's not much use to me.

I stop the image and analyse the clothes; I get so close to the screen that the light hurts my eyes. I close them, and open them again. At more of a distance, I press play and pause several times, trying to slow down the image. A black skirt, a white shirt with a black blazer, and knee-length white socks.

A realisation shakes my mind, and a small light bulb turns on. I've found something. The woman is dressed up in a work uniform, as a waitress perhaps. Or as a maid. I rub my eyes and say out loud, 'An erotic fantasy.'

The music diminishes and disappears. The woman's shirt falls to the ground and her naked body is still against a dark background. My legs have fallen asleep, and as I stand up I feel dizzy at first, but the image becomes clearer from a distance. I blink several times and clear my vision. There is the mysterious woman.

Or so I believe.

My heart falls to my stomach and joins the flock of bats. I cover my mouth in horror and freeze the image. What am I seeing? It can't be true. It's impossible. My own eyes are deceiving me. Tiredness is playing a trick on me. I stand rigid and press the play button again. I cross my arms and with my right hand I press the remote control tightly on my arm as if I were pinching it to wake up from a bad dream.

The video continues.

I wanted to know who the mysterious woman was, and now I know. She is in front of me. I have the answer to my question, but it is not the answer I was looking for.

The mysterious woman has hardly any breasts or hips. There is hardly anything. She is very young. Too young. She approaches the person behind the camera and then disappears. You can hear some banging and her groaning. Some obscene moans.

A strong chill shakes my body. My legs are a toy tower built from small wooden blocks, about to fall. I bend my knees. The tape reaches its end and I fall on the carpet. I squeeze my eyes and mouth hard and try to swallow my own vomit.

She is a girl of about eleven or twelve.

A child.

28

Thursday, 12 January 2006
Time: 4.11 p.m.

WHY WOULD someone want Uncle Paddy to keep that videotape? Maybe it was someone close to him. Someone who had absolute trust in my uncle. And why would Uncle Paddy keep it in Dad's memory box? Would that be a safe place? Why not contact the police?

It doesn't add up.

If he watched the tape, Uncle Paddy would've contacted the police. He cared about children. He would've moved heaven and earth to save that poor child.

There's something that doesn't fit. I take a deep breath and restructure my ideas from the beginning. How do I really know that Uncle Paddy gave Dad the tape? The only proof is my father's confused mind.

Better to call the police. I'll give the tape to Sergeant Jones, although it makes my stomach turn sour just thinking about talking to that policeman again. What about Uncle Paddy's funeral? The police would start asking questions of Dad and me, and people in the village would find out. There are only three days left until the funeral, and that tape could be years old. A police investigation of an old videotape would stain Uncle Paddy's memory.

Should I wait?

You should not.

Where did Dad steal this damn tape from? Or who kept it in his memory box? It has to be someone close to Dad, who knows that my father doesn't even remember what year it is. When I talked to him this morning, he told me that they wanted to poison him.

Absurd.

A second chill causes a shivering in my body. I hug myself to control the shaking. Maybe it's not so absurd, after watching the tape. I crawl to the sofa and let myself fall. I'm not ready to lose Dad too.

My mobile phone rings, bringing me back to reality. This time it only rings twice, and there's no voice message.

I take the tape out of the camera, carefully and in disgust. How could such a young child be subjected to such a depraved act? I hold in my hand the material evidence of a criminal act. It's an old tape. The child must have changed … or not. Just because the tape is old, doesn't mean that the recording is old.

I put the tape back again and start rewinding. Where will that girl be now? Is she from this area? Do I know her? I take a deep breath and repeat several times,

'A school uniform.' The girl is wearing a school uniform. She is dressed in a school uniform dancing and stripping for a pervert. A repulsive, despicable and disgusting being. And what am I doing here playing detective, watching this video over and over again?

Shame on me.

Could she still be alive? Bile reflux burns my throat.

I freeze the image of the girl in front of me. It looks like a sepia photo. Quiet and innocent, she looks at me serenely, as if she could talk to me and explain who she is. There's only impotence in me. I close my eyes, squeeze them and give a long sigh. Then I take my phone out of my pocket. The missed calls are from a number I don't recognise. I call back and a woman replies.

'Mrs Evans?'

I hesitate. 'Speaking.'

'Are you at home?'

'No. Well, yes. I'm leaving soon. Who am I talking to?' I stammer.

'I am Inspector Miranda Smith, and I work for Sussex Police Do you have a few minutes?'

My heart is pounding in my chest. I turn off the lamp and look outside on the street, but there's no one there. I sit on the sofa and accidentally press the play button. The girl starts dancing to the music. A cold sweat runs down my back.

'Mrs Evans?'

'One moment, please.' My throat is dry and I cough before I finish my sentence. I try to swallow. I try to find the damn TV remote. I drop my mobile phone on the floor. I press the pause button and grab the mobile again.

'Mrs Evans, are you there?'

'Yes, I'm here.'

'I was saying that I work for Sussex Police. You've contacted my colleague, Sergeant Jones, several times regarding the death of your uncle, Patrick Brady. I would like to arrange an appointment with you tomorrow morning to clarify the situation further.'

The situation? What situation?

'Well, it's just not a good time as I'm very busy with the funeral and all that…'

My voice fades, and the frozen image of the girl attracts me like Ulysses to the sirens. There's a long, tense silence. I should hang up, but the woman's voice vibrates in my ear.

'I'm sorry, perhaps I misunderstood Sergeant Jones' message. If you don't think it's necessary, we don't have to meet. Anyway, I'd like to ask you a few questions now if you have five minutes.'

'Sure.'

'First of all, I'd like to offer my condolences for the loss of your uncle.'

'Thank you.'

'Sergeant Jones told me that you called him concerned about your uncle's movements that night. Could you explain to me the nature of your concern?'

I clear my throat. 'Well, he went out in his car at night, which seems strange because he never drove after dark.'

The image of the girl is distracting me from the conversation.

'I understand. According to the medical report, your uncle's death occurred between five and seven in the evening. At this time of year, the sun sets from four o'clock onwards, and there's natural light until almost five. Is it possible that your uncle went out in his car before that time?'

'Yes, it is possible.'

There's a pause at the other end of the line. 'Sergeant Jones told me that you were quite nervous and worried.'

'I…'

'Why do you think your uncle wouldn't have gone out in the car?'

I hesitate for a moment, but then tell her my suspicions. 'When I got to his house, it was a mess.'

'A mess? Please explain.'

'Dinner plates, a dirty frying pan…'

'Is that unusual for him?'

'And he didn't have an inhaler with him,' I add.

'I understand. Can I be direct with you?'

'Yes, please.'

'We followed protocol to the letter. If we thought there was the slightest chance that a criminal act had been committed – and here I have to be frank, let's say if your uncle was assaulted and killed – obviously the case would go to my department and we would open an investigation. Do you understand what I am saying?'

'Yes.' My voice is softer.

'Do you really understand my words?'

'Of course.' I try to raise my voice to make it sound more convincing.

'Let me ask you what evidence you have that suggests your uncle was murdered?'

'I…' I press my lips together in an attempt to bite back the words.

'Mrs Evans, I ask you again, what evidence do you have that suggests your uncle was murdered?' Her tone is authoritative.

'I don't know…'

'You don't know?'

The image of the girl is like the pillar of salt looking at Sodom. In my delirium, I seem to be having a conversation with the mysterious girl. She speaks to me and asks me for help. It'd be so easy to tell the truth. My uncle must have run away from something, and this video may be the key to that mystery. The police need to know. I can't do any more for my uncle.

'Can I be honest with you?'

If my anguish were ice, I'd be dead from hypothermia.

'Go ahead, I'm listening.'

Her encouragement gives me a strange sense of security. I swallow and look at the girl in front of me. I tell her my secrets.

'The truth is that I'm not in a good place at the moment. This isn't the time to go into details, but it's been a hard year for me. I feel like I don't know myself. I feel strange.' My words come out of my mouth like water escaping from a broken dam.

'I understand.'

'Do you?'

'From woman to woman, I understand you perfectly.'

I feel the warmth of her voice and continue. 'Sometimes I think or even act in a way that's not me. I'm surprised and suddenly I find myself in an absurd situation like in the photo shop. Well, that embarrasses me. I feel a strong resentment against everything and everyone.' I get a lump in my throat. 'And there's a little girl. A girl I don't know.' I stop for a moment. 'Are you still there?'

'I'm listening. Go on, please.' Her voice is so close that it seems to tuck me in like a mother and inspires me to be calm.

'Well, the presence of that child is here with me, but I don't want my Uncle Paddy to suffer. I want him to be remembered for his good deeds.' I wipe my nose with my sleeve. 'So, I have to do the right thing.'

'And you're doing the right thing by sharing this with me.'

A sweet silence is mixed with a feeling of melancholy and I think of Tom. I want him to be here with me. I want him to hold me and whisper in my ear that everything will be as it was before.

'You had a miscarriage, right? I'm aware of this and I understand your pain.'

Her statement awakens me from my longing and the anxiety returns. I'm a fool to believe that a stranger can understand my pain. My uncle rushed out on Sunday night and left in his car, under such pressure that he forgot one of his inhalers, and died. And what do the police do? They take me for a madwoman and pity me. The next day I find my watch broken in front of the door, and now I have a tape of a minor stripping in front of a hidden camera.

Through my tears I see the image of the girl through another prism, a clearer, sharper glass. I tilt my head towards the screen and close my eyes. A wave of adrenaline runs through my body and I feel a slight tingling in my hands. I've just found something. It was in front of me all the time and I didn't even notice it.

'Mrs Smith…'

'Call me Miranda.'

'I'm exhausted.'

'Don't worry. I won't bother you any more. And as I say, if you have any suspicions…'

'I have none. My uncle was a good person.'

'I have no doubt. Can I be of any further help?'

I tense my back and respond in a fake pleasant tone. 'Your call was very helpful. Thank you for listening to me.'

I hang up and bring my mobile phone closer to the screen. My fingers tremble. I know where to find this child. I take a couple of photos of the black blazer with the emblem of her school.

29

Thursday, 12 January 2006
Time: 8.16 p.m.

It's late and my eyes are burning. I didn't lie to the
policewoman when I told her I was tired. I'm very tired.
After the funeral on Sunday, I'll return the tape to the
nursing home and let them contact the police. If they
ask me, I don't have to know anything. I simply found
the tape in Dad's box and warned the nursing home. I
make myself a double espresso and go into Tom's office.
I'm going to find that little girl.

I turn on his computer. The screen lights up and
gives me two options – to enter in my desktop or in
Tom's. I sip my coffee and click on Tom's, but it asks me
for a password. I try his date of birth: June 1967. Too
obvious. Doesn't work. I type the place where we met:
Valencia. It doesn't give me access either. I try with my
date of birth, September 1969, and the computer warns

me that this is my last attempt, so I give up. Is there anything else Tom is hiding from me?

I access my Google account and open the file with the photo I've taken of the school's emblem, a medieval coat of arms. The image is blurred. I enlarge it and it's easier to see the shape of the coat of arms, although the colours and small details are very blurred. I turn on the printer and print the colour image in A4 size. The resolution is quite bad – the print is a blurred amalgam of pink and red ink. It doesn't work for me. I take a long sip of the coffee. It has no milk or sugar and tastes bitter. I change the print settings to black and white and adjust the image quality to photo. The details are now clearer.

I pick up a black marker from the ceramic pot and outline the lines and contours. The emblem of the school is a heraldic shield in the form of an inverted triangle. In the background, there's a lion standing upright and raising its claws in defence. On either side of the lion, four roses fall vertically. The shield is crossed by a band diagonally from right to left that catches the lion, and on the lower point of the inverted triangle is written the year 1964. I take a pin and hang the drawing on the cork bulletin board. I have a headache. I'm so tired that I don't know whether I took the drawing from a photo or drew it from my own imagination.

I give myself a few seconds, but I can't see anything clearly. I pull the sheet from the bulletin board and go downstairs to the living room. The TV is still on, in the middle of a pile of cables. I pick up the cables, turn off the TV and put the video camera in a bag in the magazine rack next to the sofa. I put a couple of magazines on top, covering the evidence of the crime.

I sit on the sofa and turn on my laptop. I go to the West Sussex City Council website and click on the education and children's section. This category is divided into primary and secondary schools. I access the list of secondary schools in the region, a total of forty secondary schools and fifteen private schools. I have another long sip of coffee and squeeze my eyes. There are too many schools. It won't be as simple as I thought.

I randomly take a look at a couple of schools, skimming the information and location and studying the students' pictures. I compare their uniforms with the girl's uniform in the video. Then I click on more schools. Not all of them have an emblem. Some of the more modern academies use a geometric figure with the name of the school on it, or reinvent the letters in a more striking way as though creating a brand for a commercial product. A few Catholic schools shape the cross or other religious symbols in different ways. The oldest schools usually have a coat of arms or something related to the area or the town. I put the drawing with the school's emblem next to the laptop on top of a cushion. A shield in the form of an inverted triangle with a lion on the warpath. The school I'm looking for might have been open for many years.

I finish my coffee and add up the search time for the first five institutes. It took me twenty-eight minutes. Around six minutes per school. I have a list of fifty-five schools altogether. This makes a total of 330 minutes or five and a half hours searching. All of this without taking into account not collapsing or fainting at some point along the way.

It's now ten o'clock at night. What if the school belongs to another region outside West Sussex or isn't open any more? Or it has another name and emblem, and all my efforts have been in vain? I bite my lip and the pain mixes with the bitter taste of coffee. I've been a coward for not coming forward and reporting the tape to the police. I still don't know why I haven't done so. Fear? Shame? Curiosity?

I decide to limit the search. I try the official website of Ofsted, the office for education standards. I type in my postcode and search in a ten-mile radius. The list is reduced to twenty-one secondary schools and fourteen private schools. That would take me just over three hours. I have to try.

It's almost midnight. I've checked more than half the schools and I'm still searching like a zombie looking for its prey. I feel disoriented. What do I do if I find the school? Will the girl still be there? What would I tell her? That someone filmed her on the sly? I grimace in frustration. I run my hands through my hair, rub my head with my fingers and go down to my temples. I close my eyes in a failed attempt to lubricate them. What if the child is no longer a child? Even worse, what if she isn't alive? My chest tightens. I should've left this job to the police before playing a cat-and-mouse game. I don't want to stain Uncle Paddy's memory. Not until after his funeral.

I keep typing until finally I sing *bingo!* and a flow of caffeine and adrenaline breathes hope into my heart, which beats faster. I've found the school. The frame of the shield is edged in red and the background is covered in navy blue. On the background the lion is golden and the rose petals are red and white. The band that crosses the coat of arms is also red, and below it says 1964: Park Academy for Girls.

My fingers move impatiently as I enter the different sections. It's a girls' school with about 800 students. I look through photos of school activities: trips, science projects, events, sports competitions and an annual theatre performance. Why did one of these girls take part in this obscene act? I can't focus on the screen any more. Tiredness is winning the battle. A million fireflies are flying around my head and my heartbeat is more distant and weaker. I close my eyes, and I don't remember anything else.

30

Friday, 13 January 2006
Time: 7.30 a.m.

I WAKE up on the sofa with my right arm extended and almost touching the floor. I'm holding the empty mug with my thumb. The laptop is resting on my stomach. My neck is stiff, and my mouth is as dry as the sole of a shoe. When I get up, the video camera is still in the magazine rack. Where is that little girl now?

The laptop has no battery. I plug it in and go to the school's website. I hesitate. I open and close my hands while looking at the school's emblem with fascination. I don't blink and my eyes become watery. Will the child be at school today? I calculate the distance from home to the school. It's five miles and 700 yards away, a total of almost eleven and a half miles there and back. I wash my face with cold water and put on my running clothes. If I hurry up, I can make it to the school by the time it opens.

The race begins.

I tie up my life like the rudder of a boat drifting in a storm at night. Shouldn't I contact the funeral director and Father Jonathan and finalise the arrangements for Sunday's Mass? Or perhaps finish the farewell letter to Uncle Paddy? Anyway, I can't stop my training. I have to keep running for the Steyning marathon. And right now, inside me, there's a stronger desire: that my uncle's memory remains intact and the truth comes out.

I get to the main street and increase my pace.

I've only participated in a marathon once in my life, ten years ago, and it was a disaster. I prepared thoroughly for five months, and in the last two months I increased the number of miles and reduced the running time. To start with, everything went as well as I'd planned. But in the last three miles my legs started to shake. I stopped and applied an anti-inflammatory eucalyptus cream and did some quick stretches, but my muscles didn't work. There were digital stopwatches indicating the time, and runner after runner was passing me. That frustrated me.

I was having trouble running, so I decided to walk and sometimes jog, trying to get back into the rhythm of the race. My muscles hurt and my body forced me to give up. For the last 300 metres, I had to just walk. I was cold. Tom and Mum were there behind the barrier. They were shouting my name and signalling me to come out, but I ignored them. Tom knew that if I didn't raise my hand or fall to the ground, he shouldn't intervene. He'd promised me that, and he kept his promise. This was a challenge I wanted to complete no matter what, and I had no intention of leaving the race, even if I had to drag myself to the end.

The reason for my defeat was clear: lack of training. I wasn't prepared for a marathon. The amount of exercise I'd done during those months wasn't enough. I should've worked harder for that day. Twenty-six miles is a lot if you don't have a rigid training plan.

If I could turn back time, I'd change certain things. It's an absurd thought full of resentment towards myself.

When I finished the race, Tom carried me to the aid station. They laid me down and gave me an isotonic drink, and a massage to relax my muscles. It was spring, but the cold I felt was very intense. It was the last year of my mother's life and I remember it as a bittersweet year. Tom asked me to move in with him. I looked at him with an incredulous smile and didn't answer. An hour later he picked me up in his arms, put me in the car and took me to his house.

The school opens in twenty minutes. I check the distance on my mobile phone. I've just over two miles to go. I speed up when I hear the squeal of tyres braking sharply in the middle of the road. I stop. I have to be more careful. I raise my hand to apologise and continue running. I have to get to the school before it opens.

Five days ago, my uncle was found dead in his car and only two days ago I found, by chance, a video that turned out to be a minor doing a striptease and making those moans. My father tells me in his madness that the video belongs to Uncle Paddy. In a small town, misfortunes don't necessarily need to be small.

I look up. The school is a block of grey-and-red

Dakota cement buildings that has seen better days. I take out the sheet I printed yesterday with the shield to check. It's an average school that contrasts with its emblem, a heraldic shield.

Dozens of girls parade towards the gate like a trail of ants, some in groups, others alone. They push and laugh and taunt each other. I see mothers following the girls to the gate and rows of cars appear out of nowhere. I move a little bit away from the road. There are many cars parked outside. All the students are wearing the same uniform as the girl in the video. An adrenaline rush runs through my body. I'm closer to her.

I stand next to the fence, cross my arms and concentrate on watching the students go by. I look for long, dark, straight hair with a light streak. A mother comes up to me and says good morning. I'm focusing on the girls. After a few minutes the woman comes forward and raises her hand to say goodbye to her daughter. I'm left alone.

I've sweated a lot and I'm starting to get cold. After fifteen minutes the tumult disappears and the caretaker closes the gate. He looks at me. I turn around, disappointed, but stop at the corner and stay a few more minutes. Maybe the girl is late. Or maybe she's sick today. Or dead. My body shrinks from sweat, cold and fear.

Better to go home. I start to run without feeling like it. Did Uncle Paddy keep the tape in Dad's memory box because he was afraid? Are there more girls? Was it fear that caused him to rush out on Sunday night? Who was he running from? I stumble and fall, scratching my hand, and my mobile hits the ground. There's no one around. My left hand is bleeding slightly and it stings. I'm a fool. I look for my phone and grab it again. On the screen there's a missed call from Katherine, and a text message.

"I'll be in Findon in a couple of hours. Please bring the death certificate. See you later."

I get up and keep running. I come home with my left hand numb and a superficial wound. Now I have to prepare to see Katherine.

31

Friday, 13 January 2006
Time: 11.07 a.m.

I ENTER the café and find Katherine sitting in a corner by the window. We're the only ones here. She's making notes in a notebook while her eyes are glued to the screen of her laptop, immersed in some work project. With her other hand she's playing nervously with a pair of vintage dark glasses. A bit pretentious for this time of year. I straighten my back a little more and slowly approach her table. Next to her notebook are two mobiles placed symmetrically next to each other. A BlackBerry and a Nokia.

'Hi,' I say.

She stands up, looks at her Cartier and squeezes my arms while sending me a little kiss that barely touches my cheek.

'You're late.'

'I've been told that already this week.'

She doesn't respond. I eventually feel as if I've been given permission, and sit down and drop my hands in my lap.

'I stopped by the funeral director, contacted the council and now I'm filling out some paperwork,' Katherine says, with her eyes on her notebook.

'Did you see Uncle Paddy?'

'Yes. I wanted to. It's been years since I last saw him.'

Is there sarcasm in her voice?

'Why didn't you come home?' I put my hand on hers. Her nails are stained with oil paint and an almost imperceptible smell of turpentine mixes with her expensive perfume. Painting relaxes her. It's the only imperfect thing in a life made to measure.

'Megan, I'm quite tight on time.'

Her eyebrows, thin and profiled, arch over ice-blue eyes, and her voice is tinged with a hint of irritation that only I can perceive. She seems to feel strangely vulnerable at home, as if she were in enemy territory.

'It's more neutral here,' I say.

'What do you mean, more neutral?' She pulls her hand away from mine and catches the waitress's attention. 'What do you want? Coffee or tea?'

'I've had a lot of coffee today.'

'Tea, then,' she confirms to the blonde-braided, smiling waitress as she approaches.

'No. Something cold.' I turn towards the waitress. 'A sparkling water, please.'

'Up to you.' Katherine takes a short breath and

raises her eyebrows again as if I've said something stupid.

The waitress nods and leaves.

'How are you?' Katherine asks me.

The Nokia phone rings. My mouth opens; I say nothing. Katherine frowns, moves closer to the screen and furrows her brow.

'Katherine Hudson speaking.' She stands up and mumbles to me, 'Work.' Then she goes outside. Her long, thick black hair bounces up and down as she moves with confident steps.

Her work mobile, the Blackberry, is still on the table. Who is she talking to? If she had called me, we could have gone to see Uncle Paddy together. I cross my arms, tilt my head back and stare at the laptop screen. The screen saver is a black background with butterflies swaying and changing shape and colour, taken from a session with Sigmund Freud.

'Here's your sparkling water.' The waitress puts down a coaster, the bottle and a glass of ice with a slice of lemon.

Katherine's image is reflected in the glass of the café window. I try to read her lips in vain – she's just making gestures of affirmation. I pass my hand over my forehead. I feel hot and take off my cardigan. I take a sip of water and look at the screen of flying butterflies again. I lean over and slowly approach it. Their attraction is almost hypnotic. My heart speeds up as I slide my index finger over the cursor and, by magic, the screen lights up like a revelation. My breath cuts off and my eyes widen – it's the website for the crematorium in Findon.

'Well, well.' Katherine's voice catches me off guard. 'Your curiosity has been sharpened over the years.'

She's standing behind me. I don't say anything. Her face shows no surprise. She sits down while keeping her eyes on me and slowly closes the laptop screen.

'Megan, I can't stay much longer than twenty minutes before taking the train back to London. I have a board meeting this afternoon.'

My eyes dance from her face to the BlackBerry on the table as I run my hand through my hair. I'm hot.

'I understand.' I take out of my bag the frame with the picture of Mum, Katherine, Uncle Paddy and me at summer camp. 'Look what I found at Uncle Paddy's house.'

'What is this?' Her hands reach for the frame but stop before taking it.

'We were so young, and you look so pretty. Uncle Paddy used to call you Katy. Do you remember?'

My words leave my mouth like dominoes about to fall in a row. Katherine plays with her fingers, trying in vain to remove the remains of the paint on her nails. She says nothing. I want to believe that the ice in her eyes is starting to melt. I need to get her on my side..

'You look so much like Mum when she was young,' she says. 'It was a very hot and humid summer. So sticky that my watercolours didn't dry well.'

'Do you remember the girls from the river?'

'I remember more than you do.' She's still focused on the paint stuck on her nails.

'What about Juliette, the French girl who stayed with us that summer? She left before the end of the walk.

The other girls told me that she made up an illness and her mother came from France to pick her up. She was as pretty as she was weak. Poor Uncle Paddy was disappointed by her lack of gratitude.'

'Megan, I need the death certificate signed by the coroner.'

'What did you do with those paintings?'

'You're not listening to me.'

'They were such beautiful paintings.'

'Megan, your cheeks are red. Are you okay?'

'Don't you remember?' I insist.

'I do remember. I have a better memory than you.'

'And?'

Katherine squeezes her lips together tightly and her eyes seem to be hiding some kind of pain. She brings her index finger to her mouth and licks a drop of blood from a cuticle she's just torn.

'I burned them,' she answers.

'You burned the paintings?'

She takes a napkin and dries the small wound. 'Megan, they're expecting me in London. I have a lot of work to do.'

She puts her notebook and laptop in a leather briefcase as she gets up, then pulls on her black coat.

I watch her. 'What do we do with Uncle Paddy?'

'We burn him too.' Her voice is sharp and the pain in her face has gone.

'Katherine!'

'We bury him, Megan. Although it'd be more practical to cremate the body. I already called the funeral director this morning; you're in charge of the Mass.'

'Katherine, wait a moment, please. There's something I'd like to tell you.'

She looks me up and down and hands me some napkins.

'I don't have time for the same old things. What's with all the sweating?'

I ignore her offering, put the picture back in my bag and take out a handkerchief. I dry my forehead and finish my glass of sparkling water.

'A headache. Here you are.' I hand her Uncle Paddy's death certificate.

She quickly takes it and looks at it before putting it in her briefcase.

'Listen to me, and wake up. I know that Uncle Paddy appreciated you, but life goes on and it's not good to be anchored in the past.'

'And he appreciated you too. It's just that his death doesn't make sense. If you let me explain—'

'Uncle Paddy stopped appreciating me when I stopped being one of the little sheep in his flock, like you were.' Katherine is back to scratching the paint off her fingers. 'He could never have imagined I'd accept the offer to lock myself up in a boarding school in Ireland. Away from everyone and everything. One less problem for him.' Her voice is stronger, and a happy smile covers her face. She sighs and continues, 'And for the record, it was that bloody summer—' she's hitting my bag with the frame inside '—when Uncle Paddy stopped calling me Katy.'

She kisses me goodbye and walks out the door with the same fury as she hit my bag.

What was her real reason for coming to Findon? She could've made all those calls from her office in London. She came to see Uncle Paddy's body.

I'm still standing by the café table. Still. No one else is here. This is how I feel with Katherine, like that little piece of skin that rises from the flesh right beside the fingernail and causes discomfort and pain. A sheen of sweat covers my forehead again. I take a deep breath and hold it for a few seconds. Katherine has spent half her life angry and resentful towards me. I know why. Of course I know why. I know what lies behind that haughty and distant attitude: envy. Katherine adored Uncle Paddy until I took him away from her, and she never forgave me for it.

With my fists, I squeeze my bag more tightly. I feel the frame pressing into my chest. It's mine. I'll always have a piece of Katherine with me. Because I love her. A knot forms in my throat and I try to cough, but it doesn't go away. Maybe I'm just a silly girl full of sentimentality. Or maybe I'm not a good person.

32

Friday, 13 January 2006
Time: 12.41 p.m.

'I would like to cancel a bank account.'

I put my bag on the only counter that is open at the bank. The cashier, a mixed-race woman with such perfect make-up that it's impossible to guess her age, asks me in a silky voice, 'You are not happy with us?'

'It's my uncle's.'

'In that case, he has to come himself.' A strong smell of sandalwood perfume marks her territory.

'My uncle passed away and I'm doing the paperwork.'

'Oh, I'm so sorry.' She opens her eyes wider, but no wrinkles appear. 'Do you have a copy of the death certificate and some photo ID?'

I take the documents out of my bag as she watches me. 'Here's a copy.'

'You're one of the girls working at the Thomas Cook travel agency, right?'

'Part-time,' I answer without enthusiasm.

'My cousin did her training there some years ago, but she wasn't offered a contract. There were too many staff.' I nod and she continues, 'She decided to go solo. She set up her own travel agency in her husband's town.'

The sound of the keyboard mixes with her words. She turns and loads paper in the printer from a swivel chair.

'I've already told her, people are buying online now. It's cheaper.' I nod again. 'Do you know if there are any vacancies?'

My mind is not in the office. 'I don't think so. They've already closed several branches.'

'It's all right. She can always work in a bank. You need to complete this form and sign here and here.' She points with red porcelain nails as long as the claws of a cat.

I look at the documents with the name of Patrick Brady and sign next to the cross. It's been a week since I last saw my uncle. He was chatting with Dad in the greenhouse in the nursing home, showing him a miniature of the Petronas Twin Towers in Malaysia, and Dad was listening with interest. I was in a hurry to get to work and didn't want to bother them. The next day, Uncle Paddy called me to confirm whether I was going to see him on Saturday. I had plans with Tom, who was going on his trip, so I couldn't. And that was my last goodbye. Should I have gone?

'I would also like a statement of account.'

She nods and continues typing. There are ads on the wall showing newer mortgage rates. It's increasingly easy now to take out a mortgage to buy a flat, although there are rumours that these bargain rates won't last long. On the right, an electronic display board shows the currency exchange rate in blue and white digital numbers, and under each counter, there's an ad with a young couple with frozen smiles and a bank adviser: 'Invest your money more safely.'. The ads are the ultimate expression of deception.

The cashier hands me the statement of Uncle Paddy's account. I check the column with the expenses from the last two weeks. Electricity, water, council tax... When I reach the end of the column, I see a withdrawal of £150. It was the last transaction.

'Excuse me. What is this withdrawal?'

'Let me see.' She takes the bank statement with her porcelain nails. 'It's from a cash machine.'

'And the time and day are correct?'

'I think so. Sunday at 5.34 p.m.'

'This Sunday at 5.34 p.m.?'

'That's what it says here.'

'Is the time accurate?'

'Well, I don't know, really. Do you want me to ask my manager?'

Why would Uncle Paddy take out that money before he died?

'If it's not too much trouble?' I put on my best good-girl face.

She gets out of the swivel chair and seems to lose

height. She moves slowly, but with the precision of a dancer about to go onstage.

I check the bank transactions from previous weeks, but there isn't any other withdrawal of that amount of money.

The cashier returns. 'The manager told me that the hours are usually exact. Unless there's maintenance, which is usually done at weekends.'

'Was there any maintenance on Sunday?'

'Yes, there was, but not at that time. It's done in the morning.'

Was there someone with him? Someone who forced him to withdraw the money? A robbery, perhaps? The paper of the account statement gets wet with the sweat of my fingers. I lower my hands and dry them discreetly on my trousers. Can I wait until Monday to contact the police?

'Do the cash machines have cameras, like in the movies?'

'Do you mean a security camera?'

'Yes.' My voice goes up a few notes.

'Of course, all cash machines have security cameras.' She points with her index finger to the four corners of the ceiling. 'Look, here, there and over there too. And we also have alarms. There's no escape here.'

I stretch my legs and straighten my back as if it could make me think more clearly. 'Which cash machine did my uncle withdraw the money from?'

'I can't tell you that.' She crosses her hands and puts them on the counter. The red nails look even longer. She plays with them and asks, 'Why do you want to know that?'

'Simple curiosity. There aren't many cash machines around here.'

'You're right.'

'Is there any way to find out?' I insist.

'I guess there would have to be a request from the police or something like that. I have no idea, really. May I ask why you have such an interest?'

'Curiosity, really.' I press my lips together so hard that I can't even muster a smile. The police would only intervene if they had a compelling reason. And in Uncle Paddy's case, they don't have one. Well, they don't at the moment. I'll give them one.

'Do you want to cancel the direct debit payments as well?'

'Cancel everything, please.'

'You'll have to contact the electricity and water company, the council and the telephone company…'

'Did you say the phone company?' I repeat loudly, having a eureka moment as a bulb turns on in my brain.

She nods very slowly and looks at me with surprise. 'Yes, the phone company too. Should I put it all in this envelope?'

'Yes, please.'

I put the papers and money in my bag next to Uncle Paddy's mobile phone. An old Samsung.

33

Friday, 13 January 2006
Time: 1.12 p.m.

THE SMALL PHONE shop is lined with thousands of coloured phone covers, which create the illusion of entering a clairvoyant's stall in an amusement park. The dark-skinned salesman greets me with a foreign accent.

'You look like you need a mobile phone.'

His charcoal-black, carefully shaved moustache widens, tracing the smile on his face, and his eyes shrink and disappear into thick grey eyebrows.

'I look like a desperate woman, I know, and I hope you can help me.'

He stands still like a wax figure. Seconds later, a laugh breaks the silence and I jolt back a few inches. He takes a deep breath and, with a long, thin-lipped smile, responds in a teasing tone, 'I'm sorry, I'm married.'

Did he just make a joke? I take Uncle Paddy's mobile phone out of my bag and put it on the counter.

'I'm married too. I need your help with this mobile.'

'Is it yours?'

'Let's say it is.'

'And?'

'Can you unlock it?'

'You don't remember the pin code?'

'No.'

'Let me see.' He picks up the phone and examines it. 'This mobile is old.'

'I'm very fond of my mobile phone,' I say.

'A beautiful young woman like you with such an old mobile phone?'

I get closer to him. 'I'll be honest with you.'

'I'm all ears.' He crosses his arms and rests them on his scrawny belly.

'It's my husband's mobile phone. I think he's having an affair and I want to know who with. I'm desperate and I won't take no for an answer. How much is this joke going to cost me?'

I feel a slight distancing from myself. My words sound eloquent to my ears and my voice is sharper. What is making me change? Premature menopause? The search for the truth about my uncle's death? Finding the girl from the video? They all have a common denominator: loss. The loss of youth, the loss of a loved one and the loss of innocence. And amidst so much loss, I dig through the mud to recover the past. I want to know the truth and no one is going to stain my Uncle Paddy's memory.

His smile disappears, and his little eyes fix on me.

His voice is serious. 'If you're bluffing, it'll cost you £20, but if you're serious, I'll do it for free.'

'I think this is my lucky day. It's not going to cost me anything.'

The black line of the moustache widens in an upward curve and an expression dawns in his eyes that says: this is business. 'As you wish.'

He plugs the mobile into a computer then presses the central button of the mobile at the same time as he presses the volume. As if by magic, the phone screen turns into a row of electric-blue digits on a black background. He turns the phone on again and puts it in front of me, then turns his head to the side and says, with the tone of a magician asking a volunteer from the audience to choose a card, 'Type in a four-digit number, but don't tell me what it is.'

Two thousand and six, this year, the year of Uncle Paddy's death.

'Done.'

He continues with his show.

'Perfect. The mobile is now unlocked and has a new pin number. Here you are.' He returns it to me and says jokingly, 'Would you like me to guess the new number?'

His question makes me smile. I touch the mobile phone and find it cold. My heart speeds up like a car engine and changes to third gear.

'No, thanks. What do I do now?'

'Go to the main screen and look at the last incoming numbers. Like this.' He presses the main buttons while I hold the mobile eagerly.

The screen shows my mobile phone number, and

others. They all have someone's name: Father Jonathan, Megan, Anthony's nursing home…

'What about this weekend?'

He shows me the numbers again. 'There's one that has no name.'

'Who is it?'

'It has no name, I told you.'

'Let me see the number.'

My heart goes into fourth gear. I don't recognise the number.

'When was the call made?'

'Your husband called that number on Saturday morning and they called back a couple of times on Sunday.'

'What time?'

'At five twenty-two and again at five fifty-eight. Where were you at that time?'

On the fourth mile or maybe on the fifth? 'I was running. Do you have a pen and paper?'

The salesman makes a theatrical turn and puts paper and pen on the counter. I dry my sweaty hands on my trousers and write down the phone number.

'Can you find out whose number it is?'

'Miss, I'm not the police.'

'Can you check if that number appears more times?'

He presses a button and moves the screen down. 'The phone only stores numbers from the last month, and I can't see it again. Why don't you call it?'

My heart jumps in my chest and my cheeks warm. I have the vertigo of a car in fifth gear about to jump over a broken bridge. I take out my phone, but I can't dial the number. Are my fingers shaking in hesitation at jumping over the broken bridge? I press the first number very slowly so I don't make a mistake. Each digit I dial is a shot of adrenaline to my heart, which accelerates like a racing car. I put the phone to my ear without touching the earpiece. First ring. The salesman watches me while he plays with one of his rings. Second ring. What does he think of me? Does he feel pity for me? I turn my head and look down. Fourth ring. Will I recognise the person's voice? Fifth ring. What will I say? Maybe I have the wrong number. Eight rings later, I look at the salesman and shake my head. I hang up. His expression of disappointment mirrors mine.

I try again.

Nothing.

The salesman and I bow our heads simultaneously. I put my phone slowly on the counter and lean against the glass. My eyelids droop. Seconds later I say, 'What if I look in the phone book?'

He gives a long snort and responds without much enthusiasm. 'If it's a mobile phone, I don't think you'll find the owner's details in the phone book.'

'Well…'

'Why don't you call from your husband's phone?'

I squeeze Uncle Paddy's phone hard and start to perspire with the adrenaline of a driver who is definitely going to jump off a broken bridge. Why didn't I think of that before? I extend Uncle Paddy's phone so close to the salesman's face that it looks like he's going to eat it.

'Where do I press to make the call?'

He shakes his head and holds up his hands.

'Wait.' He puts a hand over mine and slowly lowers it to the counter. His hand is warm and decorated with several gold rings that contrast with the light chocolate colour of his skin. 'Not now,' he says in his clairvoyant's voice. 'If you call now from your husband's phone, whoever didn't pick up the phone when you called before, may be suspicious and won't answer now.'

'What do I do then?'

He grunts as he looks into the void, searching for an answer. 'Try again later from your husband's phone.'

'Later? How much later?'

'Wait until the evening.'

I take a deep breath and check every muscle in my body as though after falling off a roller coaster. I keep my back straight and take out my purse.

'Thank you very much. Please let me pay you for your help.'

'No, I won't hear of it. Good luck to you.'

34

Friday, 13 January 2006
Time: 2.11 p.m.

WHILE WAITING until the evening to call the mysterious number, I think I have now found a way to find out who the girl in the video is.

Behind the counter in the Oxfam shop, Sophie is sitting reading one of her magazines.

'Sorry about the other night.'

She looks at me, confused. 'Hi, sweetie. How are you? I'm reading a very interesting article about the logic of forgetting.'

Her comment upends my plan to apologise before asking her for a favour.

'And what is the logic of forgetting?'

'Something like the saying "who loves you well, will make you cry", but you don't cry if you don't remember.'

'Why wouldn't you remember?' My curiosity turns to disbelief.

'Because it has to do with your subconscious. It's a survival mechanism. Do you want to read the article?'

I try to get my head out of the clouds and start my apology again.

'I'd like you to remember the other night, because I was a little on edge and I want to apologise. Sophie, I'm not having a good time.' I tap my fingers on the counter.

'I didn't take it personally. I didn't even remember. See? The logic of forgetting. Besides, you're always in a hurry, but today we're going to have tea.'

Tea was not in my plan, but I say nothing as she makes us a cup each.

'Look what someone brought into the shop.' She points to an old metal washboard. 'You don't know this, but when I was a child, my grandmother used a board like this one. When they brought it into the shop, I didn't know what was inside the box. The sound it made simply irritated me. But when I opened the box and found the board, I remembered how my grandmother used to make me clean the house when I was a child and Mum was sick in bed. I didn't even remember that until I heard the bristle brush hitting the metal board again. See, an example of the subconscious and the logic of forgetting.'

She ends her speech with a big smile on her round face framed with golden curls, although I didn't quite understand what she was saying.

'And that happens only with noises?'

'I suppose it could be noises, smells or sensations. I

don't really know. The subconscious is wiser than we think. Do you want the magazine so you can read the article? It's very interesting.'

I take a sip of the tea and leave the cup on the counter. 'I just stopped by to apologise. I really have to go.'

'But you just got here.'

'What time is it?'

'Almost half past two. But girl, where are you going in such a hurry?'

I close my fists and straighten my back. 'I need to ask you a favour, but please don't ask me any questions.' I say it so quickly that I don't have time to process my own words.

'That sounds like an American movie and I don't like it one bit. What's the favour?'

'I need a coat.'

'A coat? All this mystery for a coat? Do you want to go shopping?'

'No, no. I need a second-hand coat. I want to buy one from here.'

'Honey, what are you saying?'

'I need a small coat. For an eleven- or twelve-year-old girl.'

'An eleven- or twelve-year-old girl? I didn't know you had nieces.' She stretches out her words, looking at me with concern.

I take a deep breath and close my eyes. I can't hide the truth with my eyes open.

'Please don't ask me any questions. I'll explain later. Can I buy a coat?'

Sophie remains silent. She gets up, approaches the coat rack and shows me one. 'Is this one good enough for you?'

'It's perfect. How much is it?'

She takes my hand. 'Nothing, honey. For you it's free.'

'Thank you. Now I have to go.'

'Megan,' Sophie calls after me, and I turn around. 'Promise me you'll tell me what's going on.'

I go over quickly and kiss her goodbye. 'I promise.'

And I go straight to the school.

35

Friday, 13 January 2006
Time: 2.56 p.m.

I GET out of the taxi and ring the bell at the school gate.
A small red light comes on and someone looks at me
through the intercom camera. Without her saying
anything, the gate opens. I walk to reception, mentally
going over what I'll say. Behind the counter there are
two receptionists in their fifties. One has short, dark
brown hair and an excess of red lipstick; the other, with
a vacant expression, has blonde hair with so many high-
lights that it's difficult to guess her original colour.

'Good morning, I'm bringing this coat—'

The blonde receptionist raises her index finger and
points to her partner while reciting through her headset
in a monotone, 'Park Academy for Girls, how may I help
you?'

I turn to the receptionist with the short hair and red

lips, who echoes, 'Park Academy for Girls, how may I help you?'

'Good afternoon, I'm bringing this coat that belongs to one of your students. She left it at the station.'

'Oh, thank you.' She takes the coat and checks the label for a student's name, but there's nothing written there. 'These girls don't even know where their heads are. They lose everything. They'd lose their heads if they weren't screwed on.' She presses the button on her headset again. 'Park Academy for Girls, how may I help you? Yes, just a moment, I'll put you through.'

She takes off her headset and pays attention to me. 'I'm sorry, you were saying?'

'I said that I brought this coat—'

'Thank you, I'll put it in the lost property box and see if one of the girls claims it. The temperature is supposed to drop again tomorrow.' She ignores me again and speaks through her headset. 'Park Academy for Girls, how may I help you?'

I step along the counter and try my luck with the other receptionist. 'I can give you a description of the girl so it's easier to find her.' She looks at me as if she doesn't understand, so I continue, 'I'm sure her mother will be very happy. It's going to be colder tomorrow.'

The short-haired receptionist intervenes. 'We'll send a general message to the students' tutors that a coat has been found. You've been very kind.'

I persist. 'The girl is not very tall, around eleven or twelve years old, with long, straight dark hair with a white streak on the right side. I'm sure you know who she is.'

The two receptionists look at each other and the red-lipped one says to me, 'Can I have your name, please?'

'Megan Evans.'

'Are you from the area?'

'More or less. Findon.'

The short-haired receptionist says, 'But Findon is more than five miles away.'

The blonde receptionist gives me a bland smile and adds, 'Sure.'

As if 'sure' explains everything. They look at each other again. What are they thinking? Have I screwed up? I take a step back, but before I turn around and run out the door, the short-haired receptionist asks me, 'Would you like to speak to the head teacher, Mr Wright? I'm sure he can help you.'

'Yes, of course.' My voice rises slightly.

She dials a number and waits. The blonde receptionist blinks several times and feigns a smile like a receptionist in a cheap hotel.

'Linda, can you put me through to Mr Wright? There's a lady here called…'

She looks at me.

'Megan Evans.'

'Megan Evans,' she repeats.

Should I have given another name? The receptionist continues, 'She's looking for one of our students.'

A drop of sweat slips down my forehead. I touch my fringe and pretend to be calm.

'No, she's not a parent. Wait a minute. Relative maybe?'

I shake my head.

'No, neither.' After a short silence, she continues, 'No…' Then she hangs up. 'Please take a seat. Mr Wright will be with you in a moment.'

What were they telling her on the other end of the line? I adjust my coat. Maybe it's better if I go.

'I can come by later.'

'No, please.' She copies her colleague's smile. 'Mr Wright is a head teacher with values, and our motto is "Students of today, leaders of tomorrow".'

That doesn't make much sense, but then I don't have much to lose. I take off my coat and sit down. Two girls pass by in the corridor. Neither of them is the girl I'm looking for. Her friends, perhaps?

With the precision of a Swiss watch, Mr Wright comes out the door to meet me. His dark suit and maroon tie look like a second skin. With a wide smile, more like a car salesman than a head teacher, he welcomes me.

'Mrs Evans?' He shakes my hand gently, with intense eyes. 'I'm Andrew Wright, head teacher of Park Academy for Girls. Would you like some coffee or tea?'

'I'm fine, thanks. It'll only take a moment.'

If I play my cards right, I'll leave the school with the name of the girl. And when I have her name, I'll be closer to the truth. Not even the police will be able to refute the real reasons for my uncle's escape from the house. Will his death have a deeper meaning?

The head teacher sits in a black leather office chair that looks more like a throne with wheels. He invites me to sit down. Between us is a large oak desk that matches his small leather throne and, on the desk, an object rests in each corner: a plaque with his name and position in gold, an office telephone, a computer screen and a classic green lamp with a small handle on the side.

'What can I do for you?' He's playing with a silver pen while staring at me.

'I found a coat at the station that belongs to one of your students and I thought I'd bring it.'

'Thank you very much for your altruistic gesture.' He keeps his car salesman smile.

'The girl isn't very tall, and she has straight black hair. Quite long.'

Mr Wright nods. 'You are very observant. Where did you say you found the coat?'

'At the station.'

'And what do you do? If you don't mind me asking.'

'I work in a travel agency. Do you know the student?'

'I know all my students. Here our motto is "Students of today, leaders of tomorrow".'

'Yes, I've been told. Well, I thought if I could take a look at the girls' photos, I might be able to tell who left her coat at the station.'

'I guess by taking a quick look at the photos we can see who she is.'

My heart beats faster.

'I would be very grateful. She is a student with dark straight hair and has a white streak on her right side.'

'You have a great capacity for observation,' he repeats with a slightly condescending tone, 'but I have another question.' He pauses as if he were in a class and wanted all the students to pay attention. 'If you could see one of our students so closely, I wonder—' he clears his throat before continuing '—why you didn't give her back her coat yourself. You said your name was Mrs Edwards?'

'Mrs Evans,' I correct him. 'Well, I didn't see her that closely. When I was getting off the train, she was coming in. I mean, when I was getting on, she was getting off the carriage, and I assumed that the coat on the seat was hers.

'And you're certain you can recognise her now?'

'Yes, yes. I waved to her from inside the carriage, but the train started and she didn't see me.'

He nods repeatedly in assent at my coherent explanation. The innocent voices of the girls from the playground reach out to the office and give me strength to continue my efforts to find this girl.

'I suppose you went back to the station to come here to the school?'

'I recognised the school's emblem on her blazer and came back.'

The head teacher touches his temple as he mentally summarises my story.

'You have plenty of time, Mrs Evans.' My neck is getting tighter. I don't answer, and Mr Wright continues, 'Unfortunately, our school has a somewhat different process for finding the alleged owner of the missing coat.'

'I understand.'

'I'm glad you understand me.' His words are slow and measured as if time were infinite inside his office. 'My secretary informed me that the coat doesn't have a flap with our student's name on it. This is unlikely, though not impossible.' He smiles. 'So, we will send an email to all our tutors so that the student can pick it up at reception. If the coat really belongs to one of our students… It's that simple.' He slaps the table and the dry sound stops my breath and my cheeks turn red.

'I understand, I understand,' I repeat, and look at the doorknob.

'If I understood you correctly, you'd like to see the photos of our girls to identify who left the coat, not at the station, as you said before, but inside the carriage.'

'Well…'

I get up and he continues in his slow, authoritative tone. 'What you're asking me to do, Mrs Evans, is against our child protection policy.' Another uncomfortable pause. 'Do you understand what I'm saying?'

'I didn't know that.' I force a smile. 'Now I know. Don't worry, I don't want to take up any more of your time. I'm leaving now.'

I feel the coat and try to find the buttons while pretending to be calm but my fingers tremble. He doesn't get up. I go out swiftly, looking at the floor. As I pass the reception, I hear the two receptionists whispering something.

I'm such an idiot. Of course they wouldn't let me see the pictures of the girls.

Does the girl from the old video have a direct link to Uncle Paddy's death? I know she does, but I can't explain how. It's as if my uncle whispered in my ear, 'Find the girl and you'll find me.'

36

Friday, 13 January 2006
Time: 4.17 p.m.

FROM THE KITCHEN WINDOW, I can see Oliver stacking boxes on his doorstep. Is he moving? I make some green tea, put my coat on and go outside.

'What are you doing?'

He turns and puts a box down next to the door. 'Organising Amy's things. I'm going to put them in the garage.'

'I'm glad you made that decision. I made you a cup of tea, if you want it.'

He takes the mug and smells it with curiosity.

'I don't have any alcohol today,' I say.

'Don't worry. I did the shopping this morning. It helps me to sleep.'

'It also helps the liver to age.'

He takes a sip and his face turns sour. 'What is this?'

'It's green tea. Organic. It cleanses the body, like

you're doing now with Amy's things. I can add sugar, although I don't recommend it.'

'No, it's okay.' He takes another sip.

At the end of the street, on the corner, a man is trimming branches that are overhanging the fence of a house. He stops and watches us. His silhouette looks familiar.

'Oliver, look over there. Who's that trimming trees?'

He puts his cup on top of a box and has a look.

'It's Peter, the local gardener.' He raises his hand to greet him.

The gardener waves hello back, but I look down.

'I've never seen him around here.'

'He does gardening work here and there. He doesn't say much, but he works hard.' He keeps his voice low. 'He had meningitis as a child.'

'Does someone look after him?'

'I don't think so. He normally works for the town hall. And he takes care of the grass at my school a few times a year. He's harmless as a child. Do you want him to give you a hand in your garden?'

I shake my head.

Suddenly there is pain in Oliver's eyes. 'I'm selling the house. I'm leaving.'

His words are a bomb in my ears. 'Leaving to go where? What about Jamie?'

'Amy's mother wants to control everything. But my son is mine, and he will come with me wherever I go.'

'Sure.'

'Maybe I'll move north.' His voice swells with hope.

Why the sudden change? 'What about your job?'

'I can always find a teaching job elsewhere. Megan, listen, too many people know me. I'm tired of being pitied. I need to get out of this environment.' He lights a cigarette.

'I understand.'

'What about you?'

I gather my thoughts. 'The funeral is on Sunday and my sister Katherine is taking care of the paperwork.' Beyond that, I don't have much else to say.

'How is your sister?'

'Set in her ways, as usual.'

'And Tom?'

'Travelling. He'll be back soon.'

Oliver doesn't ask any more about Tom. 'I cleared out Amy's office. All her things are in boxes.' He takes a puff on the cigarette. 'In boxes … like her,' he says bitterly.

'You left her some beautiful flowers.'

'How do you know that?'

'I guess I miss her too,' I say without thinking.

He nods and the light from the entrance of his house falls on his face and mixes with the smoke of the cigarette.

'I don't know what to do with her belongings.'

'You could donate them to Oxfam like I'm doing with Uncle Paddy's things.'

'I could…'

'How do you feel about packing away Amy's things?'

'Sometimes empty, other times angry, like a fury that burns inside me. Strange, isn't it? As if the rage were stronger than the sadness.' He throws the cigarette on the ground and steps on it hard.

I couldn't agree more.

He finishes his tea and hands me the mug. 'I found Amy's work diary.'

There's a silence, as if he's waiting for me to say something. I don't answer, so he continues,

'On Thursday the seventh of July she had a meeting scheduled at work. An important client, for a new marketing campaign. Some American home brand, I think.'

I take a step back with his mug. 'Oliver, you have to stop thinking about it.'

'It's the same meeting she originally had scheduled for Wednesday, the day before.'

It wasn't a good idea to come. I'm too curious. 'Maybe it was another meeting as part of the project.'

'No. It was the same meeting. She postponed it to Thursday, her day off. And I don't understand why, because it would've been a hassle for her to have the meeting on that Thursday instead of Wednesday, since we were leaving for France the next day, Friday.'

'You're right, I remember your holiday plans. Amy told me she wanted to escape the routine.'

'She postponed the damn meeting to Thursday.' His voice is getting louder.

'Something must have come up at work,' I say with a calm tone. 'But don't give it any more thought.'

'Or something came up here in Findon.' His words fall like hail from the sky.

'Oliver, I don't remember. Maybe Amy wasn't

feeling well that Wednesday, so she postponed the meeting.'

Suddenly the coat is too hot, and I open it slightly to give me room to breathe.

'She didn't stay home on Wednesday. Jamie was at nursery that day. I went to pick him up myself when I finished school. When I got home, she called and said she was on her way home from work. I made dinner. I remember perfectly.'

'Didn't you just say she didn't go to work?'

'Exactly. She lied to me. She didn't go to work that Wednesday and she didn't stay home either.'

I have to stop him. 'Oliver, I'm very tired. I just came by to say hello. This conversation is going nowhere. You need to calm down. I understand that dealing with Amy's things is painful, but to doubt that she loved you is a big mistake. Besides—' I take a deep breath and leave the air in my lungs for a few seconds before I continue '—she isn't coming back.'

'I don't doubt that she loved me,' he answers with disdain, 'but for some reason she cancelled the damn meeting in London that Wednesday. She lied to me. If she hadn't cancelled that meeting, she would still be alive with me today.'

'No, Oliver.'

'What do you mean?'

'I mean that one cannot control one's destiny.'

He comes up to me and grabs my arms. His hands are strong; I feel like a prisoner.

'Why did she cancel that meeting? You know why.'

'How would I know?'

'She was your friend.'

'Oliver, you need to calm down. Let go of me.'

'Did she have a lover? You have to tell me.'

'What are you saying?'

'Megan, I know she wouldn't have cancelled a meeting if it weren't for a good reason. Something happened and I have the right to know.'

'What do you want me to tell you? Whatever happened, Amy's not coming back, Oliver. That's the harsh reality.'

His hands fall and I escape from his clutches. I turn around and step off the pavement without saying a word.

'I'm sorry, Megan. I'm really sorry.' His voice sounds far away.

I say nothing and keep walking.

'And thank you!' he shouts as I finish crossing the street.

My hands are shaking. I turn around and my gaze meets his on the other side of the road. I say nothing.

'Thank you for listening to me.'

'Oliver…' I barely move my lips.

'And because I know you're lying too,' he shouts angrily. 'Whoever that bastard is, Amy was with him that Wednesday.'

My breathing stops short. I go into the house and lock the door. I lean my back against the door and slowly slide down to the floor. Amy is here with me. She looks at me with her angelic eyes and smiles at me. Now I understand the sudden change in Oliver's attitude. His spite is stronger than his sadness.

But he doesn't know that Amy didn't stay with that bastard.

'Amy stayed that Wednesday because of me, Oliver. So that you could continue to live in ignorance.'

I take out the broken watch from the hallway table. It's still stopped at 6.47 p.m. on Sunday night. I squeeze it hard as I squeeze hard the absurd promise to keep Oliver happy in his ignorance.

I pass the watch from one hand to the other. Now I know who brought it back. It was Peter, the gardener I just saw, the same gardener who was at the church when I visited Father Jonathan. But I still don't know why he left it at my front door. What game is he playing?

There's a message from Tom on my phone.

"You're not picking up the phone. I'm sorry about your Uncle Paddy. I'm coming home tomorrow."

Who told him about Uncle Paddy?

37

Friday, 13 January 2006
Time: 4.57 p.m.

I PLAY WITH MY PENCIL, scribbling and shaping the mysterious phone number that I've already written a dozen times in my notebook.

Tomorrow I need to tidy the house, do some shopping and pick up Dad from the nursing home. On Monday I'll contact the police to show them the video and photos. Will they take me seriously or will they take me for a fool? The video speaks for itself. There's no doubt about it. Or is there?

It's almost five o'clock. The time has come.

I pass Uncle Paddy's phone from one hand to the other. It's an old Samsung. In the last few years, he spent more time in Malaysia than here, so he only used a prepaid mobile phone. I go back into the message folder. There are only texts with the balance. I called several phone companies, but they told me the same thing as the salesman at the mobile shop – they have no data from that phone in their system.

Someone called twice, and the duration of the first call was almost three minutes. But why didn't Uncle Paddy have the number saved on his mobile? Was it someone close or someone he didn't know? What did they talk about? I come to the conclusion that the person was calling from a new number. That would explain why Uncle Paddy didn't have the number saved.

I google the phone number and scan the results. The first link that appears is a page where you can report the number. It's full of ads. I scroll down. There are links with Chinese symbols. I try googling different combinations by adding spaces between the numbers, or searching for the first four digits or the last four digits. There's nothing that can give me a clue. I look in the Yellow Pages. After payment, they send you information about the number. I enter the data and a message informs me that the phone number is not registered. What a scam.

Uncle Paddy's phone sits in my sweating hands like a hot potato. If I call the number ... what do I say? I don't have to say anything. I just want to hear their voice. I have the advantage that the person won't know who I am. But what if it's someone I know? I put my hand on my heart. What do I say? "It's Megan, Patrick Brady's niece, how are you? I guess you already know that you called my uncle an hour before he died, and I wanted to make sure you didn't kill him." An icy chill takes hold of my spine. Should I pass the information to the police? After the little attention they've given me, maybe it's better not to. I'll wait until after the funeral.

The person won't know who I am if I don't say anything. I press redial and a hundred butterfly wings brush the inside of my stomach. One, two, three rings. My heart feels like it's going to jump out of my chest. At the fourth ring, someone answers.

'Hello. Hello? Are you there?'

It's the delicate voice of a woman. My breath is cut off and my lungs are stuck. Even if I wanted to respond, I can't get the words out. I hang up and throw the mobile phone at the futon, far from me, as if it were a volcanic stone burning and melting between my fingers. Who is the woman? I haven't heard that voice before. She has a high-pitched voice and an accent. She's not from this area, but she and Uncle Paddy knew each other. She thought he was calling her. "Are you there?" Doesn't she know he's dead? How can she not know when they spoke for several minutes on Sunday night before he rushed out of his house? Bile turns my stomach. Did she warn him about something?

I pick up the mobile phone and fall into the futon. I curl up in the foetal position and let the minutes go by. The phone is a burden loaded with secrets that nobody cares about but me. The police don't listen to me. The people at the school thought I was crazy. Sophie doesn't understand me. Do I understand myself?

The mobile phone rings, but no call appears on the screen. It doesn't vibrate either. I'm confused. It rings a second time. On the third ring my blood freezes. It's not Uncle Paddy's mobile, it's mine. I jump from the futon to the kitchen counter. The mobile is next to my laptop. It keeps ringing. Is it Tom? Sophie? The nursing home? I grab it and the answer appears on the screen. Heat in my stomach reaches my cheeks. I blink and adjust my vision. I look around for my notebook. When I compare the two phone numbers, I want to disappear. The same number that called Uncle Paddy the night he died is now calling my phone. The woman knows me.

38

Saturday, 14 January 2006
Time: 5.57 p.m.

'WHAT WOULD you like to have for dinner, Dad?'

He's sitting on the bed in the guest room looking at the wall like he's watching TV.

'Dad, I'm talking to you. What would you like for dinner?'

He doesn't answer. I'm not a great cook, so I'll heat up soup from a can and make a salad.

Someone knocks at the door.

'Shh…' I say to Dad, who stays even more quiet.

I tiptoe out of the room and downstairs to the front door. Someone is knocking again.

'Megan! Meg! Are you there? Open the door.'

It's Tom. He's back early. I would've preferred to talk to him after the funeral. Who told him about Uncle Paddy?

'Meg! It's me.'

'Yes, I know it's you.' I open the door halfway. 'What do you want? Don't you have your keys?'

'I want to come in, if you'll let me.'

I open the door and we go into the living room.

'Who's this?' Dad asks as he drags his feet into the room.

'Good evening, Anthony. How are you?'

'Who are you? Megan, who is this man?'

Tom puts his suitcase down and looks at me with surprise.

'Dad, it's Tom. Don't you remember him?'

'Tom?'

'My husband, Dad,' I say, confirming the obvious.

He looks Tom up and down. 'Boy, how are you doing with your studies?'

'Good, good.' Tom's voice sounds more like a question than an answer.

I walk up to Tom and whisper to him, 'Dad's having a bad day. Go with the flow.'

Tom wears the same cologne year after year. A mixture of wood, leather and lavender. He only uses it on special occasions and never finishes the bottle until I give him another one the following year.

'What are those shopping bags?'

'I brought some dinner. I thought you might want to—'

'Eat with you?'

'Meg, we've hardly seen each other for weeks. When I'm home, you're not, and vice versa. You don't answer my calls either. I know you want your space. I respect that.'

'You said it.' I cross my arms, creating a barrier between us.

'Do you want me to leave?'

Tom plays with his ultimatums. It's been over twelve years since I fell for those blue eyes, that black hair now sprinkled with the colour of salt, and that easy, playful smile that didn't take life too seriously.

'You can stay, you can make dinner and then you can go to the couch.'

I've also learned to give ultimatums. There's no smile on his face. Is now the moment that he takes his things and leaves?

But he doesn't leave. He puts the bags on the kitchen counter and goes to my father.

'Anthony, come and help me prepare dinner.' Dad follows him like a child. 'Would you like a glass of wine? This is a Rioja Gran Reserva. You won't find this in a supermarket around here.'

They both go into the kitchen. The two most important men in my life, so far away from me at the same time. My arms lose strength and collapse by my sides.

'How are your studies going? When do you finish?' asks Dad.

'I've finished already, Anthony.'

'When I was young, only women cooked. Any man who cooked was a sissy.'

'Dad, don't be rude.'

Tom ignores my comment. He got tired of convincing me that I'm the only one in his eyes. Tom plays along with my father. He knows what he is like.

'That's good, boy.' Dad nods as he takes another sip of the wine. 'This wine is great.'

'I'm glad you like it. I have a couple more bottles in the car. They're for you and Megan.'

'Megan, come to the kitchen! Have a glass of this wine.'

'I'm fine, Dad. I'll wait for dinner.'

Dad is finishing the day much better than he started it. He gets up, grabs the bottle and pours himself another glass.

'Tom, son, do you want more?'

'Not now, thanks. I'll have more when I've finished preparing the chicken breasts.'

'I'm going to my room,' I say. 'I have to organise some things.'

I look at them, but they ignore me. Tom is cooking with his back to me, and my father is sitting on a chair fascinated by the show: cutting, chopping, frying.

As I leave the room, I hear my father say, 'When are you going to make an honest woman of my daughter?'

'An honest woman?'

'A decent man has responsibilities. I don't want to see my daughter swanning around like a tart.'

He doesn't remember that we're married. I ignore the absurd conversation and go up to my room. I sit in the desk chair and play with the little videotape. Where is the girl? What is her life like? Is she alive? Only an unbalanced person could abuse an innocent child. What if Uncle Paddy found the culprit, and that's what cost him his life? If I found the girl, she could tell me who it was, and I could find that monster. I have to try, for the memory of my uncle.

'Meg!'

I jump off the chair. 'What are you doing there?' I shout at Tom.

'Dinner's ready.' His voice sounds like an apology.

'How long have you been standing there?'

'I just got here. What's the problem?'

'You should've knocked on the door.'

'There were never any secrets between us, Megan.'

'Hardly ever,' I reply with resentment.

He looks like he's about to say something, but prefers to ignore my comment.

'You know things have changed,' I say.

'I know.' He looks down. 'That's also why I've come. Shall we have dinner? I promise I'll leave later.'

I follow him. My father is already sitting in the dining room, opening another bottle of wine.

'This wine goes down like water.'

'But it will take a while to go out,' I say.

Tom laughs at my comment.

'I know what you're planning, Tom,' I say. 'You want us to be alone.'

He just smiles at me. He offers me a chair like a gentleman, and I sit down. My father fills my glass. I say nothing. Who am I kidding? I need wine tonight too.

'Bon appétit.' Tom carefully places the chicken pieces and the garnish as if he were painting a picture.

'Weren't you supposed to be away until later next week?' I ask him.

'I had a couple of presentations in Belfast tomorrow,

but I cancelled them. One of my colleagues will do them for me. Someone called me and ... well, we'll talk later.' He looks down at his plate.

Who called him? Tom wouldn't cancel a work commitment for anyone. His job is his passion. A passion much stronger than our relationship. I take a long sip of wine.

Tom keeps talking to my father like he used to, as if the years haven't passed. He's very charming, which has always created some sort of insecurity in me. I take another sip of wine.

'Dad!'

He's had too much to drink and can't stay upright at the table.

'That's it, I've had enough.' I take the cutlery off him and wipe his face with a napkin. 'You'd better go to bed.'

Tom gets up and helps him.

'You stop playing along,' I say irritably to Tom. 'The party's over.'

Tom doesn't say anything. He grabs Dad by his arms and takes him to the guest room. He takes off Dad's clothes, puts on his pyjamas and lies him down in bed, all while answering his silly questions.

I stand still by the door. What do I feel for Tom? Love? Anger? Resentment? I don't know. Feelings are not an exact science; they're more like a broken compass.

He closes the door, turns around and says to me, 'Megan, we need to talk. You have to tell me something.'

'That Uncle Paddy died, and the funeral is tomorrow?'

Tom shakes his head gently.

'I already know that. It's something more important.'

39

Saturday, 14 January 2006
Time: 10.06 p.m.

It's after ten o'clock at night. We're sitting at the dining room table, opponent against opponent. We stare at each other. The wine warms my veins and leaves my head adrift. There's a fictitious calm in the air. Something is going to happen, but I don't know what.

This silence has the taste of the prelude to a battle.

'You start.' I give Tom permission to begin his attack.

He looks at me and makes a gesture like he wants to get up but can't, and then relaxes his muscles.

'How are you?' he asks.

'Fine. Is that what you wanted to know?'

'Your uncle passed away.'

'Is that why you came back earlier than planned? I didn't mean to break your plans.'

He ignores my comment. 'Well, I knew that me being away would give you some space.'

'You're not doing it for me. You're doing it for yourself. I don't need you to be at the funeral. No one will notice your absence.'

He looks up. 'Are you sure?'

'I've never been so sure,' I lie. 'What do you want me to do? Get into a time machine and pretend nothing happened?' I bite my lip and it gives me a pleasant pain.

'No, Megan, I don't want that. I'm going to go and leave you alone, but I need to know that you're okay.'

I sigh. 'What do you want to know?'

'How is your father?'

A crooked smile escapes me. 'He's reliving his youth. He confuses people like he confuses the tenses. Sometimes he talks to me as if I were Mum, and with you … well, you've seen it. He thinks we're still sweethearts. He's happy in his ignorance. He's happy.' I repeat it to convince myself.

'And your marathon?'

'It's going well.' As paradoxical as it sounds, Uncle Paddy's death has given me the strength to run even more.

'And the funeral is tomorrow?'

'I told you. Yes, it is, but I don't need your help if that's what you're trying to say. Katherine, the super businesswoman, is taking care of the paperwork and making sure everything is finalised as soon as possible. I'm taking care of boxes and other housekeeping chores. Do what you want.'

'And you're okay?'

227

'I am. I guess I am.'

'Sure?'

'I'm sorry, what is the point of this interrogation?'

'I don't know, I was wondering if you have any anxiety—'

'I'm telling you I'm fine.' I take a deep breath and finish my glass of wine. 'Tom, this is the third time I've asked you why you're here. You hardly knew Uncle Paddy. He was already spending long periods of time in Malaysia when you and I met. If you feel that you had to change your travel plans because of my uncle's death, I can assure you that I had no expectations. You shouldn't have bothered.'

'You don't expect anything from me?'

I look away. 'Give me time.'

Tom gets up from his chair and looks through the kitchen window, with his back to me. He fills a glass of water and drinks it in one go. Then he sets the glass on the counter and drops a bomb. 'The police contacted me.'

I open my mouth, but the words don't come out. He turns around and his look pierces my soul.

'Do you understand, Megan? The police contacted me while I was in Belfast.'

'Police? Why?' I stammer.

'You tell me.'

'Why you? I don't understand.'

'Megan, I'm your husband. You are Mrs Evans, like it or not. Are you going to tell me what's going on?'

'I don't know what you're talking about.'

'Megan, please.' He raises his voice. 'I was told

you've been calling the police about your Uncle Paddy's death. That you insist he was murdered.'

My gaze is lost on the ground. 'What did you tell them?'

'What could I tell them?' He lifts his hands in the air.

'What did they tell you, then?'

'They asked me questions about our situation. Your medical history. Your miscarriage, and other things I don't remember. It took me by surprise.'

'Is that why you came?'

'Yes, Megan, that's why I came.'

'When did they call you?'

'Yesterday afternoon. After you ignored my messages, I planned to leave you alone and contact you on my return. But I was surprised to find out from the police that your uncle had died.'

'I wasn't sure, and…'

'You don't have to justify yourself. It seems that we both like secrets equally.'

'What did you tell them?'

'That in my opinion you're fine, and that we're just going through a marital crisis at the moment.'

'Thank you.' My voice cracks.

'But you know that I now doubt the first thing, and the second thing is not true. This moment has already lasted far too long for both of us.'

His eyes change to the colour of the glass. He turns around and fills it with water again.

'That wine has made me very thirsty.'

'You know how much I loved my uncle. Maybe I

didn't accept his death when they told me. I refused to believe that he had died, just like that. I didn't have anyone to talk to either. You know the wall my sister has created between us over the years. And, well, Dad is here, but he's not.'

'I understand.'

'So, after accepting the circumstances, I've been making arrangements for a few days now.'

My whole argument sounds plausible. I've just told him the truth. Not the whole truth, but I haven't lied either.

'And there's nothing else?'

'No.'

'Why did you go to that school?'

A punch of adrenaline hits my stomach.

'What?' I can't hide the surprise in my voice.

He turns and stares into my eyes. I'm helpless.

'You heard me. The police told me that you went to a school looking for information from one of their students. The head teacher contacted them and that was the reason they contacted me.' He clenches his fists. 'A stranger showing up at a school asking about a minor sets off an alarm. They wanted to confirm with me that you're stable. I didn't know that you were into investigative journalism now. Megan, what's going on?'

I'm speechless. Stupid me.

'Nothing. Nothing is going on,' I say abruptly.

'Megan, I've reassured them that you're perfectly fine and that I'll take responsibility for you. I have to contact them again after speaking to you. I'll tell them that you're going through a difficult time, a very sad moment for you, of course, and you're in the process of acceptance. That I don't have the slightest doubt of that.'

Suddenly all my anger turns to grief. 'Tom, you have to go.'

'Megan?'

I raise my hands, creating a wall between us. My legs are shaking.

Tom crosses his arms. 'There's something else before I go. Something about us.'

'Your final confession?' I say, swallowing my grief.

He sits down and sadness envelops the room. Something very serious is about to happen and I don't know if I'm ready.

'I've been doing some thinking, and I've done the maths,' he says.

'I don't understand.'

'You had a miscarriage six months ago. In the last five months I've been working an average of fifty-two hours per week and have been away thirteen times on work trips. More than a month all together.'

'Where are you going with all these numbers?'

He raises his hand for me to listen. His easy smile died the day our baby died.

'Let me say what I've come to say, please.' He gathers himself and continues, 'A couple of months ago I got all prepared, and since then I've been thinking about which path to take. This last trip has given me the answer.'

'Thinking about what?'

'For months, you've suspected me of an infidelity

that never happened.'

Burning metal nails twist in my stomach. 'Tell me something I don't know.'

'And you've rejected me for many months now.'

'I lost my baby, Tom!'

'No. We lost our baby.' He stresses the last two words. 'An accident in which I was also affected by your suffering, our suffering. Time stopped for both of us and I've tried to be patient.'

'No, you have not.'

He says nothing, and neither do I. A silence opens up as big as our wound.

He opens his suitcase and takes out some documents.

'You're not here, Megan. You haven't been for too long, and the loss of our child has fed that loneliness. Remember that, regardless of the damage I've done to you. I take responsibility for my faults, but remember that this culprit also had an accomplice: you.' He points his finger at me.

Then he gathers his things and goes to the front door. When he opens it, the cold mixes with the sadness in a meaningless void. I hear his car pull away in the darkness of the night and I'm left alone with my punishment. He won't spend the night on the couch at home.

The foundations of my life are crumbling like desert sand. The assumptions that surround my existence are no longer true. This is the darkest night of my life. And at the dining room table, where we spent so many nights eating and laughing, Tom has left his last words: the divorce papers.

40

Saturday, 14 January 2006
Time: 10.37 p.m.

I OPEN MY EYES, but the divorce papers are still there along with the dirty dishes from dinner. I swallow and pathetic denial becomes a sad reality.

A copper lamp hangs from the ceiling, less than a metre above the centre of the dining table, illuminating the document. I lean forward and the light illuminates me too. It looks like a big light bulb in a theatre during the most dramatic scene of the performance. Everything around it is dark. The actress is alone onstage and the audience is watching her expectantly.

I run my fingers through the pages and when I read Tom's name and mine, my fingers tremble. I hold the document close to my face and take a deep breath. I rub my fingertips against the print. The ink is fresh. I flip through the pages quickly and breathe in the smell of the moving sheets. It smells like freshly printed paper.

Has Tom really been preparing the divorce for months?

A rage in my stomach is gasoline about to ignite. I throw the papers with all my strength, but they don't get very far; they swing scattered in the air and glide gently to the floor. I open my mouth, but I can't scream. On the floor rests a manual with instructions for my new life.

I clench my teeth, clench my fists and stamp the ground. I hate you, Tom. My body tightens up. I constrict each and every one of my muscles, from the smallest to the biggest, and hold my breath. The blood hits my temples and produces a buzzing of bees. My heart beats more and more slowly. My vision closes like a tunnel without light at the end, and a slight dizziness takes me away from reality. I close my eyes. A tingle expands through the pores of my skin and loosens my soul.

Is it the best thing for both of us?

Yes.

No.

I don't know.

My body is asking for air. I cough loudly. I hold my hand to my heart and gasp in a long breath. Then I breathe again. And again. I'm getting closer to the answer. And the answer is that yes, it'll be best for both of us. I get up and walk away from the lamp. My hand drops and an uncontrolled tear slips down and stains one of the sheets of paper.

The curtain falls, and me with it.

I have no other choice. I know what I have to do.

I put on my leggings, jacket and trainers. I check on Dad and leave home. The night is cold, and the cold is dark. I run in the solitude of the night. My blood comes to life again, warming my muscles. I pass by the cemetery and stop for a few seconds. Amy is there. She's dead. My stomach twists in disgust and guilt. I keep going, as if running will help me to escape. As if running will help me go back in time. When I arrive at the police station, I give myself a couple of minutes to catch my breath, then go inside.

A small policewoman in her fifties, with short white hair, is turning the pages of a Sunday magazine under the light of a dozen fluorescent tubes, looking bored.

'I'd like to speak to Sergeant Jones,' I say.

The message I've prepared is a bombshell: my uncle was murdered, and I have evidence to prove it. I put my fists on the counter, lean forward a few inches and focus on the policewoman, waiting for an affirmative answer.

She examines me from top to bottom as if measuring the consequences of a possible attack, and says in a firm voice, 'Firstly, good evening. I am Constable Daniella Collins. Secondly, Sergeant Jones is off duty. It's very late. Can I help you with something?'

'Can I talk to someone about my Uncle Paddy?'

'You can talk to me. Who's your Uncle Paddy?' Her look is inquisitive.

'Patrick Brady. He was found dead inside his car last Sunday.'

'And you're his niece?'

I nod, dropping my hands and shoulders.

She closes the magazine, comes around the counter

and puts a hand on my arm. 'You're soaked in sweat. You'll catch pneumonia. Sit down.' I obey, and she continues, 'I'll bring you a towel. Would you like something to drink? Tea?'

'Water, please. Water will do me good.' I'm trying to justify my state. 'I'm preparing for the marathon in Steyning.'

'It's good you keep yourself fit. I used to run when I was younger too.' She lifts her chin. 'I ran several marathons in my youth.' She hands me a towel from an adjacent wardrobe and takes a plastic cup from the water cooler. 'Cold or natural?'

'Cold, please.'

She takes a deep breath and presses the cold-water dispenser. 'Aren't you too young to already have hot flushes?' She passes me the water.

'These aren't hot flushes. They're more like fireworks.' I finish the water. 'Can hot flushes affect the memory?'

She closes her hand and rests it on her cheek, considering her response.

'Stress does. For example, a woman suffering from post-traumatic stress after being raped can experience gaps in her memory. Even when it's a failed attempt at rape. Fortunately, we haven't had any cases here in recent years. We're a very small police station.' She sits next to me. 'You didn't come here to talk about sexual assault, did you?'

My stomach twists as if I had swallowed a snake. I have clear symptoms of déjà vu. Do I feel like I've been here before? Yes. Memory gaps? Also yes. Memory of intense feelings? Intense and negative. I feel as if I were inside the film *The Matrix,* where everything is a lie and déjà vu is a failure in the system and a warning sign of imminent danger.

I take shelter inside the towel and look at the floor. 'I have some information I'd like to pass on to Sergeant Jones.'

'What kind of information?'

'Information on my uncle's death.'

The policewoman takes the empty cup from my hand, leaves it on the counter and comes a little closer. Her voice is a whisper. 'Did you contact the funeral director?'

'The funeral is tomorrow.'

'But tomorrow is Sunday.'

'It's a Catholic Mass.'

'Okay. And you have everything ready?'

'My sister has taken care of the paperwork. When can I talk to Sergeant Jones?'

'You're telling me you have information in relation to your uncle's death. What kind of information?'

'Confidential information,' I say. 'Are you going to tell me where Sergeant Jones is?'

My question is impatient and borderline rude. I bite my lower lip as if punishing myself for my impertinence.

Her smile deflates. 'I told you that he's off duty.'

'What about someone else who's handling the case?'

She blinks nervously. 'No one is handling the case because there is no case. If you tell me what the information is, maybe I can help you.'

I get up and the towel falls at my feet.

'Is the case filed?'

'Mrs Evans, we deal with criminal cases, not civil ones. Would you like to tell me what this is about?'

'I told you. About my Uncle Paddy.'

'Take this.' She passes me a tissue. I didn't even notice that a few tears have crossed my cheeks.

'I have proof that he was murdered.'

It takes me a few seconds to become aware of my words. I don't know if I said them out loud or in my mind until she reacts to my distress call.

'Are you aware of what you're telling me?'

I nod several times and then shake my head. 'I'm no longer aware of anything, if I'm honest.'

'Murdered?' she repeats in an echo.

'I don't know what to think any more.'

She moves my hair and lifts my chin. 'Look, you were telling me that the Mass is tomorrow.' I nod, and she continues, 'Go home. Try to get some sleep and I'll pass the message on to Sergeant Jones, okay?' She keeps looking at me and repeats, 'Okay?'

I barely nod.

'I'll call you a taxi,' she says.

'No. I'm from this area. I'll run home.'

'Are you fit to run?'

'It's the only thing I can do. Running relaxes me.'

41

Sunday, 15 January 2006
Time: 12.11 a.m.

I ENTER THE HOUSE. Dad's peaceful snores from the guest room fill the void. Not even a bomb would wake him up. I put the video camera in a bag from the supermarket, and in another small bag I put the videotape with the photos of the girls in the river. I wrap the small bag with so much tape that Sergeant Jones will have to use pliers to open the package. Then I go upstairs and into my room. After taking a shower, I prepare my clothes for tomorrow – black trousers and a matching black jumper – and leave them on the chair. I leave the farewell letter to Uncle Paddy, which I'll read during the Mass, next to it.

Tomorrow everything will be over. And when it's all over, I'll leave everything and find a new life.

My stomach roars. I go downstairs to the kitchen and open the fridge. There are leftovers from dinner. On the counter there's the third bottle of wine Tom brought. I pour myself a glass and devour the rest of the chicken. The divorce papers are still on the floor. I take a deep breath and feel needles pricking my lungs.

I call Tom. He picks up the phone, but there's no answer.

'Tom, are you there?'

After several seconds of silence, I hear my name.

'Megan.' His voice is slow and thick. 'Is that you? Is something wrong?'

'No.'

'No?' he says with confusion.

'I'd like to ask you something.'

He snorts. 'And you can't wait until Monday?'

'I can't even wait until tomorrow.'

His silence makes me think about the past. What was the first of the many mistakes that marked the beginning of our end?

'Tell me.'

'Do you remember when we used to go camping?'

'I do.'

I take a deep breath. 'What would your ideal forest look like?'

'Megan, what are you talking about?'

He doesn't call me Meg any more.

'Your ideal forest,' I insist.

'Do you know what time it is?'

'I'm just asking you to describe your ideal forest. I need to know.'

My voice is hurried, but the delay on the other end of the line tells me that he's thinking of some excuse not to participate in this game. I take the bottle of wine, fill another glass and drown my sorrows.

'Tom, I shouldn't have called you. I…'

His voice returns. 'My ideal forest?'

'Yes. The forest of your dreams.'

'I don't dream any more, Megan.' A long silence becomes a grief that shrinks my heart. 'My forest is full of trees of different heights and sizes living together in groups.'

'As a happy family?'

'As happy families.' Then he pauses for a moment. 'Does that make sense?'

'It makes sense to me. Is it day or night?'

'Megan, are you drinking?'

I hold the phone between my shoulder and my ear while I pour another glass of wine. I've been drinking more this week than the whole past year. I raise my glass to the light and confirm to myself what's obvious.

'Does it matter?'

'It matters that you are well.'

'Let me be, please. I'm just having a drink. Day or night?'

'There's an intense morning light.'

'And the path?'

'What path?'

'The path you're walking on.'

'Hmm… You've been on that path. It's a straight, defined path, without large stones.'

I drink the whole glass in one go. A toast to the path. My stomach fills up with alcohol that anaesthetises my pain.

'Now you have a big problem. You meet a bear.'

'A bear?' He starts laughing. It's not a laugh of joy, it's more of a melancholic laugh. A laugh painted with the colours of nostalgia. 'It's a Care Bear. Do you remember that cartoon series? I used to watch it with my sisters when I was a child. I loved it.'

'A Care Bear?' I repeat with surprise.

'Each one had a different symbol on its belly with a special power: love, joy, tenderness…'

Is that the way Tom sees his problems?

'And the pot?'

'You didn't mention any pot. But if I were to fantasise, I'd say that the pot would be made of gold and silver, big and expensive.'

'You've always had a good relationship with your family and your younger sisters.'

'They're lovely. They ask me about you. What does that have to do with a pot and some bears?'

According to Sophie, it has a lot to do with that. 'What about the hut?'

He is suddenly quiet and I can only hear his breathing. My head is spinning.

'Tom?' I long for his voice.

'Megan, I think I've already answered a lot of questions. I need to sleep. You need to sleep.'

No, I say to myself. I know what you need. You need to put distance between us, but you still miss me.

Now I'm the one who doesn't talk.

'Megan, listen to me.'

'I won't bother you any more.'

But he persists. 'Stay in the house as long as you need to. I'm in no hurry to sell it.'

'Tom, I have to go.'

'I know, me too.'

The call ends, and my heart falls to the ground and hits the divorce papers. I finish the bottle while deciding whether to pick them up from the floor or go straight to bed. Someone knocks gently at the door. The kitchen light is on. I try to get up, but I can't. I try to focus my gaze, but the alcohol is winning the battle. Care Bears? I start laughing. I finally stand up, but the silly laughter continues. Someone knocks on the door again. Is it Tom? I feel one heartbeat stumble over another, and another, until my heart speeds up like an engine in propulsion, but all I get is my senses hyperventilating with more alcohol, and the dizziness is stronger. I approach the door and call out, 'Yes?'

'Good evening. I'm Constable Martin Wilson. Can I speak to Mrs Evans?'

I don't open the door. I look through the window. It's the police.

'What's the matter?'

'Don't worry. It'll just take a minute. Can you open the door, please?'

Am I dreaming? I open it slowly, trying to straighten my back and erase the silly smile from my face. A round-faced, chubby policeman takes off his cap.

'Mrs Evans, are you all right?'

'What do you want? You're going to wake up my father.'

Even a bomb wouldn't wake up my dad. I'm overcome with silly laughter again. An uncontrollable, absurd laugh. I've seen the police more times this week than I've seen them on TV in the last year. The policeman puts his hand on my arm.

'Have you been drinking?'

I move my arm away and lean against the door frame. 'I'm at home.'

'Well, yes. I saw the light on. My partner, Constable Collins, asked me to pass by.' He narrows his eyes. 'I'm sorry about your uncle. Are you alone?'

'Didn't I tell you that my father is at home?'

'You also told us that you had some information in relation to your Uncle Patrick's death. You said he was murdered.'

I hold the door frame more tightly. My belly swells and my mouth fills with water. I lift my chin as if I could lessen the heaviness in my stomach.

'Yes, that's right,' I reply.

'Do you want us to take a statement?'

'What about Sergeant Jones?'

'He's not on duty. I can take care of it, if you cooperate.'

I don't like his comment.

'The funeral is tomorrow. Tomorrow. Tomorrow, it is, so…' My words don't have much coherence.

'I understand. What proof do you have?' he insists. He's holding a pen and a notepad.

'My imagination and a videotape. A very lively imagination, I guess.'

'A videotape? Can you explain further?'

Drunk people always tell the truth, and I'm no exception. I don't feel like laughing any more.

'I said that my imagination runs through my head like a videotape.' I put my hand to my mouth without being sure whether I'm holding in a gag or covering up a lie.

'You were told that your uncle died of an asthma attack.'

'Were you there?'

'Sorry?'

I raise my left hand in an apology but prefer not to say anything. Everything is spinning. The policeman looks at me with pity and closes his notebook.

'We'd better wait for Monday, after the funeral,' he says. 'Try to rest. I'm sorry to have disturbed you at this time of night.'

He turns around and leaves and I rush to the bathroom. The gag is like a waterfall from my stomach. I grab the toilet and vomit several times: the chicken, the wine and my misery.

42

Sunday, 15 January 2006
Time: 7.11 a.m.

'YOUR HUSBAND WANTS to know who you were sleeping with.'

I lean forward to Amy's headstone and brush away some dry leaves with my hand. Next to the grave, some naked trees intertwine their branches as if embracing each other. It's early in the morning and there's no sun or moon in the sky, just a blanket of grey clouds.

'This morning when I woke up, I had a strong need to come and see you.' I read her name carved on the white marble slab. 'And on my way here I saw the light on in your house. Your husband has become a sleep-walker like me. He checked your work diary and found a change of date for your last meeting in London. He thinks it was an affair.'

A gust of cold air makes me shiver. I forgot my

gloves. I blow hot air into my palms and the smell of death mixes with the smell of winter.

'You and I know you postponed your business meeting for another reason. A more important reason than seeing a lover.'

I sit on the old wooden bench and curl up in the corner. My thoughts fly to the past. Amy would have preferred to have her last business meeting that Wednesday so she could have more time to arrange her escape to France, as she called it. She had to make a last-minute change that cost her her life.

The days following her death were terrible. Oliver was in shock and Jamie was too young to understand that his mother wouldn't be coming home. A week later I made the same journey she had that Thursday morning. I took the bus to Brighton station, and from there the train to London. When I arrived in London, I got on the Tube to Victoria Station and sat on one of the benches by the platform where she died. I didn't know whether to feel anger, guilt or grief. I was just deep in shock. A swarm of people arrived and left as if that tragedy had never happened. I looked at my watch. It was nine thirty, the same time Amy was standing there waiting for the door of the Tube to open, juggling to get into the carriage, not knowing that her life was about to end. There was no pain. Her death was instantaneous.

'Do you want me to tell Oliver the truth about your death?'

On the Wednesday morning, Amy came to my house to drop Jamie off before going to London. When she knocked on the door, I opened it and slapped her.

Then she knew that I had discovered her secret. She stood still for a few seconds, touching her cheek. My hand was throbbing, and the tingle spread all over my arm. The silence was broken by the cries of her son. I put my hand across my belly, making small circles. Amy entered without my permission and closed the door. Jamie was still crying, and she kneeled to calm him down. She appeared to be calm and that was fuel for my anger. She kissed him and gave him a motherly smile. I told her to leave the house, but she ignored me and continued to reassure Jamie. Something twisted in my chest. Something ugly and dark. Something I never thought existed in me. Seconds later she stood up and looked through the window as Oliver left their house and got into his car. I tried to open the door, but she stopped me and tried to calm me down. She wanted me to listen to her, but I didn't want to hear any lies. Her apparent calmness shattered, and her eyes were full of tears of despair. She denied all my accusations. I didn't care. That Wednesday I was ready to tell her husband that I had strong reasons to believe his wife was sleeping with my husband.

I clench my teeth and my upper lip throbs nervously. My jaw hurts. Now I wonder how I was so sure that Amy was lying. Was she lying? Of course she was lying. The text messages to Tom's phone were obvious. The time they spent together. The complicity. Tom and Amy were up to something. I scratch my nose and swallow. I relax my jaw and let out my anger while breathing steam that blends in with the cold and disappears. What if she was telling me the truth? That there was nothing between her and Tom. Why was she so afraid that I would talk to Oliver? That morning her eyes showed fear. Fear that I would speak to her husband. Why? A twinge of anxiety pierces my back like an electric shock and brings me back to reality.

Timid rays of light break through the blanket of clouds. Within the cemetery fence, a gardener is raking dry leaves, cleaning up the path. I put my hand on my belly. I press my fingertips gently and make a small circle in a clockwise direction. And then another. From right to left. And I continue. Almost perfect circles. I hum a lullaby, but the pain doesn't leave me. My belly is empty. That Wednesday morning, a pool of blood covered my feet. Before arriving at the hospital, I had already lost my baby.

The next day, Amy died in the terrorist attack in London and I went into post-miscarriage syndrome. I never told Tom about my meeting with her. There was no longer any reason to be jealous. The jealousy turned to resentment. And now the resentment evaporates, and a fist squeezes my chest mercilessly and my heart fills with guilt. Guilt for a past that I cannot change.

It's time for me to go.

'Dear Amy, I hope you can forgive me.'

43

Sunday, 15 January 2006
Time: 7.53 a.m.

THE GARDENER WATCHES me as I stand up from the
bench. My heart races through my chest in a marathon.
We know each other. I know what he did. He looks
down and walks towards the shed, but he sees me
approaching him, and when I increase the pace of my
steps he starts to jog awkwardly.

'I know you.'

He turns around. His eyes are childlike and his
tongue falls swollen over his lower lip, giving him the
look of a hanged man.

'It won't do you any good to hide!' I shout to him.

Why was he lurking around my house, and why was
my broken watch left at the door? I run after him. He
enters the shed and closes the door. I hit the old wood
and small splinters stick in my hand. I knock as if it were
my last action in this life. And the more I knock, the

surer I am that Peter is involved in Uncle Paddy's death. My heart runs desperately up my chest to my throat and my words pile up in my mouth.

'The police know about you.'

Suddenly all is silent. I kick the door then fall down exhausted. Who was Uncle Paddy running from on Sunday night? Who is the girl in the videotape? Did Uncle Paddy give his life to save an innocent child?

'You're going to tell me what happened.'

The strength of my voice dies, and I can barely hear my own words. Will I ever know the truth? I'm alone. There's only dry leaves and cracked tombstones. Nobody knows I'm here. Panic cuts my heart with a scalpel and my world falls apart. The force of gravity makes me lose my balance for a moment. I have to leave. I tense my legs, and when I lean against the door a larger splinter sticks in my palm and a drop of blood runs to my wrist and falls on the wet ground. I pull out the splinter and the pain gives me life.

From the other side of the door, Peter whines like a child. The door clicks. The same splinter sticks in my heart and takes my breath away. My legs are ready to run away. Little Shrek half-opens the door.

'I'm sorry, I'm sorry,' he repeats with barely any voice.

Is it a trap? I take a step back and contemplate the scene. Peter puts his dirty hands on his face and cries. He cries like a child. His tongue hangs from his mouth and saliva drips onto his overalls. Do I feel sorry or disgusted?

'Why did you bring the watch to my house?'

He covers his eyes with his soil-caked hands.

'Why?' I insist.

'I found it,' he answers in a shaky voice.

'In the middle of the night?'

'I … I saw you running.'

'And you know who I am?'

He takes his hands off his eyes. They are swollen and flattened, and his cheeks are dirty.

'Mr Brady's niece.'

He tilts his head and raises his eyes towards me. I count the emotions that shine in his eyes: fear, confusion, innocence. I inhale a deep breath and my lungs fill up with the smell of mould, metal and wet soil. I take a handkerchief out of my bag and extend my arm. He takes it slowly and passes it clumsily over his face. I keep my distance, and, with a serious tone, insist, 'Tell me what happened.'

'You ran, you ran a lot. Very fast. You are very fast.' He has a silly smile and snorts.

'Continue.'

'I was standing still, by the fence, picking up the pruning tools.'

'What happened to my watch?'

'It fell and I picked it up.'

'And why didn't you bring it back to me?'

He looks at me without understanding. 'I brought it back to you.'

'When?'

'By the door.'

'You don't know how to knock on the door?'

He looks down at his muddy boots and wipes his

face with the sleeve of his T-shirt while tapping his right foot on the ground.

'I asked you a question. Please answer it.'

The tapping sound becomes more frequent and intense. His torso moves back and forth nervously.

'No.'

'No what?'

'Fear. A lot of fear.'

'Fear?' I'm trying to make sense of what he's saying. 'Fear of what? Of whom?'

His movements become more intense. 'I want to go.'

I look him up and down, not knowing what to say or do. I reach out my hand but stop halfway.

'Yes. You can go.' My voice is softer.

'I don't want any police.'

I sigh and look at him for a few seconds. This poor wretch couldn't hurt a fly, even if he tried.

'There'll be no police,' I say, shaking my head too.

Last Sunday night I suffered a horrible hot flush while running. My first ever hot flush. My hormones betrayed me, and my body was pure fire. I was afraid and ran even faster to get home, but the more I ran, the more intense the hot flush was, and the more afraid I became. When I got home, I had a big argument with Tom. The stress and fear were still there. What did Tom care about me running? I ended up so exhausted that I got lost in my own dreams and didn't wake up until the next morning.

Margie confirmed the state I was in when I came home. I remember being afraid and I also remember having the argument. But I don't remember the details. I ran too many miles at a speed I wasn't used to and the hot flush was very intense. My body collapsed. Everything was obvious: a strong hot flush that could knock down an elephant, plus another of the many arguments I've had with Tom.

But there is something else related to that night. My uncle died and my broken watch reads 6.47.

Did I really argue with Tom? Was the hot flush the source of my fear?

If I didn't argue with Tom and the reason for my fear wasn't the hot flush, whom did I argue with on Sunday night and what was I really afraid of?

44

Sunday, 15 January 2006
Time: 9.38 a.m.

THE CHURCH IS full of incense, religious figures and
shadows. Weak shadows that make it impossible for the
human eye to perceive where the darkness ends and the
light begins. Trapped in that half-light, I find myself
sitting in the front row with my back straight; Dad is
beside me. Above the altar, Jesus Christ hangs from a
cross. His eyes look at me sadly. I hold tightly to my
farewell letter and the old family photo I found at Uncle
Paddy's house. Under the altar lies the coffin covered
with a white cloth embroidered with a red cross, and on
top, an old Bible. The Mass begins in twenty minutes. I
am not expecting many people. An hour later we'll be at
the cemetery and after the burial everything will be over.

'I want to give this picture back to Uncle Paddy,' I
tell Dad.

He puts on his glasses and runs his index finger over

the photo from left to right, stopping for a few seconds on each family member: Mum, Katherine, Uncle Paddy and me. The last day of the 1980 summer camp. Dad was out of town and Mum picked us up. There were no more camps after that. Uncle Paddy moved to Malaysia and rarely visited us. Katherine lost contact with him. I kept in touch. When Mum died, his visits became more frequent. Then he came back to stay permanently.

'Uncle Paddy looks very young,' says Dad.

The weight of sadness invades my heart. 'Yes, you're right.'

Uncle Paddy was strong and slim and highly regarded in the community for his work with young people. He had the charisma and energy to move the world.

'And you look very pretty,' Dad continues.

'Not as much as Katherine.'

He ignores my comment. I put my hand on his arm and rest my head on his shoulder as if I were ten years old again.

'And Megan too,' he says thoughtfully.

'Megan?' My voice doesn't hide my surprise. 'And Katherine too.'

'Katherine…'

'Your daughter Katherine,' I insist.

His face twists into a look of contempt and he spits, 'That spoiled brat.' His voice sounds like sandpaper scraping wounds.

I look from side to side with shame. We're alone. I swallow and scold my father. 'That's not how you should talk about Katherine.'

His jaw is shaking, and his wrinkles get deeper by the minute. The silence blends with the darkness of the church and becomes unbreathable. He returns the photo to me, his eyes fixed on Uncle Paddy's coffin.

'How do you want me to talk about her? When your brother told me, I couldn't believe it. So intelligent and so stupid at the same time.'

An adrenaline rush speeds up my pulse. Dad is confusing me with Mum. What mistake did Katherine make? The official version was that she moved to Ireland to study at a very young age. She did so well in life that she became the businesswoman she is today. I have always justified Katherine's rejection of Uncle Paddy on the grounds of pure childish jealousy, but does she hold a grudge against him because he betrayed her? What did she do that I was never told about? I grab my heart and play at being Mum.

'She is still our daughter.'

'That's not the way we brought up our daughters, and you know it.' He looks up and his eyes nail mine. 'You didn't tell me anything, and I had to find this out from your brother.'

Find out what?

'I'm sorry. It's not fair.'

'Fair?' Dad clenches his fists and moves them through the air in a chaotic way. His words are propelled out of his mouth. 'It's a shame. A stain on this family.'

My body temperature is rising. 'I'm so sorry,' I say, my voice trembling. 'What would be best for Katherine?'

Dad grabs the edge of the bench and squeezes hard. His gaze is fixed on Uncle Paddy's coffin. He doesn't dare look at me, he doesn't dare look at his wife. His words are a whisper, a little secret that you only share once in your life.

'Your brother has arranged everything.' Shame and anger are mixed in his voice. 'Once Katherine arrives in Ireland, she will give the child up for adoption.'

Dad's words tear my chest, scratch my heart and burn my skin with cold fire. I want to deny what I'm hearing; I want to believe that my brain is imagining it or that he's invented it. Katherine was only thirteen years old. She wouldn't be able to do something like that. I try to come to my senses. I breathe deeply but my lungs are cement. It's the first time that everything starts to make more sense, although the form it's taking is too twisted.

I'll keep the picture.

'How are you doing?'

Father Jonathan approaches us with the smile that a priest dedicates to the family of the deceased on the day of the funeral.

45

Sunday, 15 January 2006
Time: 9.55 a.m.

THE SOUND of a pair of heels hitting the ground echoes in the church. Katherine breaks through the half-light and crosses the rows of mahogany pews laden with Bibles. Her walk is elegant, more arrogant than confident, and certainly with a touch of mockery.

'Here I am.'

She takes off her coat with the energy of a woman who has created herself. She wears a straight, fitted, sleeveless dress to match her long black hair. Her face is even more radiant than usual, and her eyes are bluer. She passes her palm up and down in front of our father's face, as if he were blind.

'Is Dad okay?'

He raises his head and looks at her with empty eyes. He doesn't recognise her. Katherine is no longer thirteen years old.

What happened to the baby? Who is the father? Was she forced? My heart beats like a tank driving uphill. Who did she meet at the last summer camp? It was just a camp for girls.

I can't look my sister in the eye.

'We're fine,' I answer, feigning a neutral voice. I scratch my cheek and notice that I've had the farewell letter to Uncle Paddy squeezed in my hand the whole time.

'And Tom?'

'He isn't here,' I reply with a don't-ask-me-why expression.

She sits down next to me, puts her leather bag in the shape of a half-moon between us and looks at her watch. The church is still empty, and Dad is still quiet. I put my hand on his leg. Katherine looks at the coffin. She plays with the remains of paint under her finger-nails and sighs too dramatically. I reach out to touch her, but I can't.

'You look beautiful.'

She ignores my comment. She's staring at Uncle Paddy's coffin. Her pupils flicker and she blinks nervously.

'Do you know what the advantage of being Catholic is, that you don't have as a Protestant?' she asks, her eyes still on the coffin.

I don't answer. I try to hide my confusion.

'The confessional,' she continues. 'God's forgiveness is given through that wooden box.' And she points contemptuously at the confessional without moving her eyes from the coffin.

I look at her, intrigued. 'Katherine, what are you talking about?' I whisper.

'When you commit a sin, you go to the confessional, confess it and the priest gives you absolution in the name of God.' She looks at me, and I feel the heat of a blush stain my cheeks. 'But when a Protestant commits a sin, you have to deal with God yourself, directly.' Her lips form a bitter smile. 'And it's more difficult for you to be forgiven.'

'Katherine, I don't understand what you're talking about.'

'There is so much that you prefer not to understand.' She stretches out every word and her voice has an uncomfortable ring to it. 'Besides, I have very ugly nails.' And she closes her hands, hiding her nails as if ashamed.

What are her words hiding?

Father Jonathan is at the altar ready to start the Mass. He raises his hand to let several people in. Three older men sit at the back and an old woman at the other end of the bench. I don't know them. Uncle Paddy moved to Malaysia more than twenty years ago and I didn't invite anyone.

Katherine looks at her watch again and digs in her bag. The little light on her mobile turns on. Father Jonathan reads a fragment of the Old Testament followed by some personal comments.

What betrayal did Uncle Paddy commit that Katherine cannot forgive?

I take out the picture of the last summer camp, and look at it so intently that the image seems to come alive like in a film. Mum is a metre away from us with the car keys in her hand. I'm holding on to Uncle Paddy's arm, and he's smiling with a silly grin and has his arm around Katherine. Katherine has one shoulder higher than the other as if she wanted to turn around, as if she wanted to sneak away, as if she wanted to… I make a nervous movement with my head to throw that thought away from me. My stomach shrinks and plummets like a meteorite. The temperature of my heart drops by thirty-seven degrees and fear freezes my body. As if Katherine wanted to escape. Escape from Uncle Paddy.

Father Jonathan raises his hand for me to go up to the altar. My body doesn't respond. My throat is dry and my eyes fill with tears.

'Here you are.' Katherine throws a handkerchief at me and I feel a chill. 'You're crying a lot for Uncle Paddy.'

My hand barely reaches the handkerchief.

'I'm crying for you,' I mumble.

She opens her mouth but says nothing. I stand up, look at Uncle Paddy's coffin and then back to her. I bite my lip and nod nervously several times.

'I know.'

She studies me. On her face I see a glimpse of something I haven't seen before, a mask that cracks. A feeling that in another state of mind I wouldn't have noticed: shame. Katherine is the most self-confident woman I've ever met. But now I see the expression on her face, the shame squeezing her heart.

I take the first step towards the altar like a prisoner approaching the gallows. I have as many knots in my stomach as pearls in a rosary. I put my foot on the second step and my body wobbles. How could something like this happen in our family? I take the third step. I put one hand on the altar and with the other I press hard on my farewell letter. In the background, the three men in dark suits and the old woman in mourning clothes watch me attentively. I think I see Tom too. Everything is spinning inside me. My fingers are shaking, and I can't unfold the letter. Father Jonathan puts his hand on my shoulder. I lean towards the microphone. Dad has his eyes on me, but Katherine has disappeared.

'Uncle Paddy...' I clear my throat. I try again but my heart closes my throat and doesn't let me speak. Who was my uncle really? The recollections with which I have built up Uncle Paddy's memory crumble and explode into a thousand shards. Now I understand Katherine's hatred. And now I also feel a rope around my neck. The same rope I felt when I woke up on Monday morning. I can't breathe. My legs are shaking, losing their balance, collapsing. Not only do I have to hold my own weight, but also the weight of the truth.

46

Sunday, 15 January 2006
Time: 10.37 a.m.

'MEGAN?'

It's Mum's voice.

'Megan, wake up.'

I open my eyes, but the light is very intense, and I close them again. Someone puts a hand at the back of my neck to help me lean forward. A strong hangover squeezes my brain as if I'd been hit on the head with a hammer.

'Drink some water. It will do you good.'

I half-open my eyes and try to adapt them to the light. The blurred image of a face comes closer and further away as it talks to me and puts a glass of water to my lips.

'Drink,' says Mum. 'I didn't know you were going through the menopause. You've sweated a lot. That explains why you're so sensitive.'

I obey and take a sip. I swallow with difficulty and greedily. I'm thirsty.

'Do you feel better?'

Katherine brushes a lock of hair from my face and leaves the glass on a little table. She's sitting next to me and I'm lying on a sofa. I mistook her voice for Mum's.

'Where are we?' My tongue is swollen.

'In the waiting room in the church. You fainted. You've been unconscious for almost ten minutes. They're taking the coffin to the cemetery.'

I open my mouth, but she leans forward.

'They won't do anything until you arrive.'

I look down and the memories flood my mind. 'I know. I know.'

'You know what?'

'I know about Uncle Paddy.'

Katherine gets up from her chair. 'Are you ready to go out?' she says as she puts on her coat.

'I need to share something with you.'

'Can't it wait for later?' She adjusts her gloves and grabs her leather bag.

'No.'

She raises an eyebrow with an accusatory expression.

'I know,' I repeat more intensely.

'You know? What do you know?' Her gaze is made of metal and before I reply, she jumps at me like a panther defending her territory. 'Megan, listen to me. Uncle Paddy is dead. D-E-A-D. Do you understand? The past is in the past.'

If her words were ice, I would've died of hypothermia. My eyes don't leave the ground and my voice is shy.

'Katherine, I think I always knew, but it was easier to see Uncle Paddy's kindness.' She takes out her mobile phone. 'What are you doing?' I ask.

'Texting Tom that you're fine and we're on our way.'

'Katherine, I know.'

'So what if you do know?' she shouts, and hits her phone hard on the table. 'What do you want? A medal?'

'Katherine…'

She turns her back on me and looks through the window. I don't move. Neither does she. Only her fingers move nervously inside her leather gloves. There's something holding her back. Seconds later, her voice gives free rein to her story.

'Mum swallowed her sorrow and Dad thought I was a slut for getting pregnant at thirteen.'

The surprise catches me, and I can only observe Katherine's silhouette in front of the window frame with her back facing me. She looks like a painter's muse. She contemplates her past through the window and undresses it with each of her words.

'The day I gave birth I was anaesthetised. When I woke up, I suddenly remembered those nights when Uncle Paddy visited my room, when Mum and Dad were away. And I felt a deep pain that someone who had cared for us and loved us deeply had acted like that. And I understood the damage he had done to me. It wasn't only his nightly visits and his evil deeds, but the deepest betrayal that a child of my age could feel. I understood why my subconscious had covered up his betrayal, covered up his depraved acts, and then I knew why I had buried them in oblivion, not remembering them until that very moment. It was because I had no choice. I was a helpless child. I buried any memory of sexual abuse in my subconscious as a survival mechanism.'

I am petrified.

She pauses to gather her strength and continues, 'After my exile to Ireland, I met Uncle Paddy for the first time when Mum died. I always found an excuse not to see him. You and Dad were on your way and I wanted to get there before you to see that monster for the first time. I entered the church, this very church; I remembered my past and I remembered him. When he saw me, he didn't recognise me at first. He was older, fatter, uglier. He disgusted me. He tried to give me a hug, but I pushed him away. I saw him weak. Weak for the first time. Or maybe the years gave me a strength I didn't have when I was young. From my mouth came the most abominable words I've ever said to a human being. The cross of Jesus was my witness. I told him that I had never hated anyone as much as I hated him, and I wished him dead. He told me that he had also thought about death. That he had prayed to die. And that more than once he had tried to take his own life. I told him that he was a coward.'

My stomach is a mixture of fire and acid. I don't even dare to breathe as she continues her story.

'A year ago, Dad called me from the nursing home. I still don't know who helped him contact me. He spoke fast and nervously. He told me that he had something going on with his mind, and although he couldn't remember things, he had done the day before. He said that he was losing control of his memory. He told me that he knew he hadn't been a good father. He spoke to me in desperation. He repeated that he'd done something horrible, something very ugly, and he didn't remember why I hated him so much. He also told me that he hoped I would forget that horrible thing too. To erase it from my memory. I told him not to worry. And he answered that he just wanted me to know.'

She turns slowly and her serenity dazzles me.

'After hanging up, I cried with sadness, but also with relief. I felt that I was a child again but this time I didn't feel guilty. I felt no responsibility for how Uncle Paddy's actions marked my childhood. Dad gave me the best words to cure my anguish – what we must remember, but also what we must forget.'

'And what was the terrible thing that Dad had done?'

She smiles at me for the first time in a long time. 'Megan, Dad understood in his madness what really happened to me. He never saw it so clearly until he entered that state.'

'But he doesn't remember you.'

'Don't be deceived.' She puts a hand on my shoulder. She looks taller. 'He chooses not to remember me.'

'What about Uncle Paddy?'

'You were once a victim of his games too, but you don't remember because you were too young.'

Her statement leaves me motionless, as if the bony fingers of a dead man caught my throat like wire and didn't let me breathe.

'Me?'

'It happened once. You were very young, and to escape was not a viable option, so I guess you preferred to erase that event from your mind rather than accept a betrayal. It's not uncommon among child-abuse victims. Not uncommon at all.'

'The last summer camp,' I confirm more than ask, and an irrational shame clutches my heart.

She nods. 'To mistrust Uncle Paddy would've meant you losing him.' Her voice has a timbre that I haven't heard before: acceptance.

Every muscle in my body is inert. I can't get any words out of my mouth. I feel Katherine's arms around me, and she whispers in my ear. 'When Uncle Paddy moved to Malaysia, I no longer had to worry in Ireland because I knew he would never touch you again.'

47

Sunday, 15 January 2006
Time: 11.15 a.m.

THE CEMETERY IS a landscape of grey tombstones sitting unevenly on a mantle of dry leaves that create a chaotic rainbow of brown.

The gravedigger and Peter the gardener surround the coffin with ropes to lower it into the grave. There's no wreath – I asked them to leave it in the church. A group of people stand around the coffin. We look like a circle of black chips from a macabre board game. Checkmate. Uncle Paddy's game has come to an end.

An arm rubs mine, looking for my hand. It's Tom. He touches my fingers, but I don't react. Nobody says anything.

A few months after the last summer camp, Katherine was moved to the boarding school near Dublin. Dad dressed up the news like it was something really good for the family, and Mum accepted it. They were proud that their bright daughter with a promising future was going to study at a prestigious Irish school. A wealthy acquaintance of Uncle Paddy's arranged it. A few weeks later, Uncle Paddy left the sacristy and went to Malaysia. Did he leave to atone for his guilt?

Katherine watches the coffin being lowered into the pit. There's no sadness on her face, no joy either. Only serenity. And inside me, pride and love for her are intertwined like branches of the same tree. Next week I'll leave my pride at home and go to London to see her and tell her important things. Because the most important things are the ones that are never said.

Why did Uncle Paddy return from Malaysia? A couple of months ago he settled permanently in the old house that the Church gave him when he moved from Ireland years before. He was old and tired. I should've believed Dad when he told me the videotape belonged to Uncle Paddy. My body trembles. I was so sure he was wrong. I hold on to Dad's arm to keep warm.

They lower the coffin into the bottom of the pit. I bend down and throw in a handful of soil. I'm still sure that something dark happened to my uncle on Sunday night. Someone had dinner with him, since I found an extra plate in the sink. What happened during dinner to make him run away in his car after dark? Revenge? Who witnessed his escape? The police found no evidence of criminality. Not in the car, not in his house. My breathing is slower. On the other side of the coffin, three men and one woman, retired teachers from the old Catholic school, pay their respects. Father Jonathan invited them, and they expressed their condolences a few minutes ago. Did they come to make sure that Uncle Paddy is dead?

And the girl in the video? Where is she? Uncle Paddy literally took the secret to his grave. Shovelfuls of soil cover the coffin and it disappears. How could I have been so blind? A chill runs down my back. The wind is cold, but it's even colder when you know a loved one is no longer with you. Or the idea of a loved one. I take a deep breath and wind up my heart.

I look up and see small lights in the air flying like fireflies. A slight dizziness clouds my vision. I focus my eyes and see the figure of a woman in the background by the cemetery gate. I blink again. The figure is still there, like a mirage. I leave the group and start walking, dizzy, to the gate. Someone asks where I'm going but I don't pay any attention. The figure is so clear that I think I'm dreaming. I speed up my pace. Reality and imagination play with my mind. It's her. My pulse accelerates like a rocket in propulsion. It's the girl from the videotape. An adrenaline rush propels me to run. She has noticed me and is running away, but I'm running faster. She looks older. I go through the gate into the street and look both ways, but she's not here. Is she the murderer, who came to laugh at my uncle? I look again and see her turning the corner.

'Hey!' I scream at her. But she ignores me.

I run after her like a hunter after his prey. I reach the corner and see her in the car park, hurriedly looking for her car keys. She's not a child, she's a very small woman with Oriental features. She wants to get away, but I'm not going to let her go. I'm only a few metres away. With the last breath I have left, I make the sprint of my life. She quickly enters her car and locks the doors. I knock on the window and shout again. She ignores me. Her eyes are fixed on the dashboard. Her mind is plotting something. I'm not going to let her escape. In the distance I see Tom, and raise my hands for him to come in a hurry. The mysterious woman starts the car. I keep hitting the window. I see my own reflection on the glass, and I get scared. I have crazy eyes. Tom is running towards us.

The woman opens the car door and shouts, 'Get in!'

I automatically jump into the car, and we drive quickly away.

'Why are you following me, Megan?'

My heart beats like a snowball down a hill. I pant so fast that I start hyperventilating and the strong dizziness creates the illusion that the car windows are a cinema screen, and my life goes into fast forward.

I don't have my bag, I don't have my phone, I don't have anything. I don't know where I'm going, and I don't know who the woman next to me is either. I only know that she knows my name.

48

Sunday, 15 January 2006
Time: 11.37 a.m.

'Who are you?' I ask.

The car smells of cigarettes and petrol. The strange woman manoeuvres the car with the urgency of a small child in a bumper car.

'Why are you following me?' She has a foreign accent, long, straight black hair and androgynous features.

'Tell me who you are. Where are we going?' I'm holding on to my seat belt like a rope on a cliff.

'Why you follow me?' she repeats. 'I don't want any troubles.'

'I want to know the truth. Stop the car. Stop the car or I'll jump.' I put my thumb on the seat belt and with the other hand I touch the door handle.

The woman opens her eyes wider when she sees my arms stretched out, ready to jump. She shakes her head and pulls off the road suddenly. The abrupt stop jolts me towards the dashboard and the seat belt brings me back to the seat. Sickness stirs in my stomach. We're stopped in the middle of a field.

'I don't want any troubles. Get out.' Her breath smells of cigarettes and a bad life.

'I'm not going anywhere until you tell me who you are and why you came to my uncle's funeral. How do you know my name?'

'It's my car. Get out,' she repeats, although her voice loses strength.

She's scared.

'How do you know Uncle Paddy?' I insist.

'You are his niece. I am a friend.'

'Where from?'

'The Church.'

'I don't believe you.'

'Don't believe me, I don't care.' She shrugs.

'Why did you run away?'

'I don't like funerals.'

She opens the glove compartment and takes out a half-empty pack of cigarettes. She puts one between her lips and tries nervously to light it with a lighter several times. Her fingers are stained with nicotine.

'That's a lie. You're the girl from the video.'

Her body freezes for a few seconds. She takes the cigarette out of her mouth, puts the lighter down and turns towards me.

'Video?'

She looks surprised. Her mouth is jagged like a

child's, although her teeth are yellowish and contrast with her apparent youth.

'I have a tape where you do a striptease.'

'There is no video.'

'You show up in a school uniform doing a striptease. Someone is filming you on a hidden camera.'

'Hidden camera?'

'"You'll be a woman soon".'

The title of the song is like an alarm clock for her and her voice goes up an octave. 'Paddy! Where is the video?'

'I have it at home.'

'How many videos?'

'I only have one.'

'I want it.'

'And I want to know who you are.'

She rolls down her window and lights the cigarette. The cold from the outside keeps me alert. The woman stares at the smoke coming out of her mouth, giving it a sensual touch, although the way she smokes is clumsy, as if she learned it recently or because she's nervous.

'Life in Malaysia not good.'

'And my uncle helped you come to England?'

She takes another puff. 'More or less. He helps poor girls in Malaysia. He looks for a home for them, he looks for food, he looks for work.'

She gestures with the cigarette between her fingers, repeatedly.

'And you met him in Malaysia?'

'Yes, when I was very young. I do services.'

'Services?'

'Men.' She takes a long puff on the cigarette.

I don't bother to hide my surprise. 'And Uncle Paddy?'

'Doing services too young is forbidden here.' She points her fingers, the cigarette almost down to the butt. 'In Malaysia, sometimes not. I can be a child with Paddy and there is no problem with the police there. He is good man.' She takes a last puff on the cigarette and throws it out the window. 'The video?' She blows the smoke out of her nose.

Am I in front of the killer? My pulse is racing. There are only fields and cold around us. I open the car door in a false attempt to stretch my legs. The woman watches me without understanding. From the outside I rest my hands on the lowered window to hide their tremor, fear and cold mixing in my body. I lean into the car.

'Did you visit Uncle Paddy on Sunday?'

Her body jumps back a few centimetres. 'You crazy.'

'Did you kill him?' My voice vibrates and my words come out of my mouth in panic.

'Crazy.'

'Answer me!'

'You know.' Her tone is lower and syncopated. 'You saw through the window, you saw Paddy, you saw me.'

Each sentence passes through the cold air between us and enters my ears slowly, with difficulty. Her words swell and distort and sound low like a demon's voice in an exorcism.

I look down in confusion, desperately searching for an explanation that will give meaning to the prostitute's words. My brain can't process what she said, and searches for some sort of memory about last Sunday.

'Liar!' I say. 'I'm going to the police to tell them you were with my uncle the night he died.'

'You listen, niece. Put the video in your front door tonight at 9:00. I pick up. No video there, I go to the police.'

I look at her with disgust. 'And what are you going to tell them?'

Her smile is filled with evil. 'I will tell them that on Sunday, you and Paddy went out in his car and disappeared. Crazy.' She starts the car and leaves.

I struggle to contain my body's response. My knees tremble and I fall to the ground, curled up like a foetus in the middle of an empty, lifeless field.

49

Sunday, 15 January 2006
Time: 1.35 p.m.

'OPERATOR, I would like to make a collect call.'

The words come rushing out of my mouth. One ring, two rings, and up to five rings. No response. With every ring my heart rate increases. With every ring, the wind blows harder. Katherine, pick up the damn phone. After the seventh ring, I hear her voice.

'Hello?'

'Katherine, I need you to pick me up.'

'Where are you?'

'I'm calling from a phone box at a petrol station on the Steyning road.'

'You scared us to death. Who was that woman?'

'I don't know.'

'You don't know?'

'A prostitute, I think.'

'You got into the car of a prostitute you don't know? Are you crazy?'

'She knew Uncle Paddy. She's the girl in the video.'

'What video are you talking about?'

'I'll explain it later. I need you to bring me my bag. I've got the keys to Uncle Paddy's car in there.'

'I don't get you.'

'I need to remember what happened in the car on Sunday night.'

'Megan, you have a lot to explain. Tom told me about the police.'

'Please come alone.' And I hang up.

Twenty minutes later and several degrees lower, Katherine arrives in her car. She's alone. She looks at me through the window but says nothing. She parks at the petrol station and approaches me with her self-confident attitude.

'Here's your bag.'

'Thank you,' I say.

She snorts. 'Megan, for the sake of your mental health, this has to stop. Leave the past in the past. You can only change the present.' Her hand catches my face and presses on my cheek. 'Look at me. You have no right to rub salt into the wound.' But I look away. She caresses my cheek and gives me a kiss. 'I'm going now.' She turns around.

'I need you to come with me to pick up Uncle Paddy's car. I beg you.'

'Can't Tom go? Megan, I need to get back to my life.'

'Only you can help me,' I insist.

'Come to your senses.' She runs her hand through my hair, giving me a firm look. 'Picking up the car won't do you any good.'

'Katherine, I was the last person who was with Uncle Paddy the night he died.' My breath dries up. 'And I don't remember what happened.'

She takes her hand out of my hair and her pupils dilate into a deeper blue. She lowers her gaze and stands there, thinking. Her silence makes me feel even more uncomfortable.

'Let's go then.'

We get into her car and I tell her all about the photos of the girls in the river, the video and the prostitute. She drives quietly, looking at the road. She doesn't nod or ask questions. I should have come to get the car earlier, but I couldn't face it. Minutes later, we arrive at the roadside where Uncle Paddy was found in his car the night he died.

'What are you going to do now?' Katherine asks.

I observe the car and get the dizziness that you feel when you're about to enter a haunted house and you wonder whether to stay or run away.

'I don't know.'

Now is when I wait for my brain to react and send some image to my mind that will clarify what happened that night. I run my fingers along the car, a green 1989 Renault 18. Uncle Paddy bought it second-hand from a friend of Tom's a few years ago. Until he moved back permanently, he only used it to go shopping and run small errands during his short visits to Steyning before returning to Malaysia again.

I open the door and sit in the passenger seat, trying to evoke a memory. Katherine gets in too.

'Do you want to take the car home?' she asks. 'Tom could take it to a dealer for scrap.'

I ignore her comment. I breathe in the car's smell: worn-out upholstery and an air freshener in the shape of a pine tree hanging from the mirror. I touch the glovebox. I open it. Inside, there are only old papers relating to the car and some sweet wrappers. Nothing. No flashback comes into my mind. I guess I've seen far too many films.

I pass my hands over the upholstery and something cuts my fingertip. I cry out in pain.

'What is it?' Katherine asks, alarmed.

'A piece of glass,' I say.

I feel the pain of a stinging wound, but no blood comes out. It's a superficial wound. I find the piece of glass and take it closer to the light. It's shaped like a semicircle. I squeeze my brain looking for a lost memory. Something. When the frustration is as great as my desire to find an answer, a spark jumps in my brain and excitement tingles in my chest.

I hurriedly take the broken watch out of my bag. Bingo. It fits perfectly.

'It's my watch face.'

'Let me see. Six forty-seven.'

At that very moment a feeling more than a memory emerges. 'Can you remember emotions?' I ask.

'What kind of emotion do you remember?'

'On Sunday night I had a nasty argument. First, I thought it was an argument with Tom. We're not in a good place,' I confess to her with a complicity I'm not used to. 'Now I know I must've had the argument with Uncle Paddy.'

'About what?'

I hold the watch tightly in my hands like a medium.

'I don't know.'

'And the watch shows the time when you hit it.' She nods.

'I remember feeling very angry.' I caress the watch. 'But I don't know what about.'

Very angry, I repeat to myself and look out the window, waiting for the answer to fall from the sky. Outside, the temperatures are dropping. Snow is expected. Katherine's voice brings me out of my thoughts.

'Perhaps because you discovered his secret.'

'His secret?'

'Uncle Paddy wasn't expecting your visit. You confused the features of the prostitute with those of a child and your subconscious reacted.'

I add the last piece of the puzzle. 'Uncle Paddy was an inactive paedophile.'

Katherine nods. 'He saw you so upset that he put you in his car, tried to calm you down like he did when we were little, and that was like adding fuel to the fire.'

It makes sense.

'I had an unbearable heat, my first hot flush.'

'And the betrayal turned to rage.'

'And the rage turned to fear. Fear,' I repeat.

My chest shrinks and my throat closes. I cannot breathe. Despite how much the temperature has dropped, an uncontrollable sweat soaks my body, and a colony of ants crawls up my back to my head, producing a dizziness so great that I'm afraid of losing consciousness. I want to scream, but I can't. I want to run, but I can't. I want to disappear, but I can't. I feel Katherine's hand touching my shoulder, and she says in an uneasy voice, 'Megan, what's going on? You've gone white as a sheet.'

'Hysteria, dread. I wanted to run away.' I look at her in despair. 'Why can't I remember the details?'

Katherine looks down thoughtfully and plays with her fingernails. She opens her mouth several times but says nothing, as if she were afraid of her own words. When she finally does speak, her voice is slow. 'To accept the situation, you had to accept the betrayal of someone you love deeply.'

'A betrayal? What do you mean?'

She continues without looking up. 'When we were kids, Mum and Uncle Paddy took care of us. Remember? Dad was away working all the time. We depended on Uncle Paddy both physically and emotionally. The day after, I didn't retain the memory of his abuse. It was erased from my mind. I erased them all so that I could still love him. I was a child. I needed him, to survive.' She pauses for a long time, looking for the right words, and her eyes twitch when she looks at me. 'The desire to cover up the betrayal was stronger than accepting the truth. An act of survival.'

I reflect on Katherine's words and make sense of my own story.

'And I survived this week by unconsciously

suppressing the betrayal, thus erasing my memory from Sunday night, so that I could continue loving Uncle Paddy?'

'I don't know, Megan.' She sighs sadly. 'It's been many years for me, but maybe that explains why you don't remember.'

I imagine my uncle's hand holding my arm tightly and me hitting my watch on the car window as I try to free myself. I imagine the skin on his face changing colour. I imagine myself running away. But the only thing I don't imagine, and that is real in me, is the emotion I felt: fear.

My heart makes a fifty-metre free fall.

'I'll never know if I killed him.'

'Megan, don't talk nonsense.' Katherine's eyes are wider and her voice louder. 'No one killed him. The police are not stupid. He had an asthma attack.'

'Dr Brown told me it was unstable asthma caused by low temperatures. Then Sophie and I searched on the internet for information on asthma.' I put my hand on my heart. 'An asthma attack triggered by an emotional reaction such as laughing or crying.'

A smile twists Katherine's face. 'I'm a bit sceptical about believing things from the internet. All I know is that you didn't kill him.'

I say nothing. I feel lost.

'Megan, listen to me. You had a panic attack. One so bad that you fell apart and ran away. So bad that you have memory lapses.' She holds my hands, and my eyes meet hers. 'You had the courage to come back. Everything is fine.' Her hands are clutching mine.

I sigh deeply. 'And now?'

'What do you mean, now? Now we're going home, you back to your life and me to mine.'

'But—'

She cuts me off. 'Megan, you're wasting your time playing with the past. What do you gain from this? Nothing. Uncle Paddy is dead, and with him died a nightmare.'

50

Monday, 16 January 2006
Time: 10.25 a.m.

JUST AS I'M about to leave home with my suitcase, mentally prepared for my job interview, I receive a phone call.

'Mrs Evans?'

'Speaking.'

'I'm calling from the dry cleaner's. You left a coat here and it is now repaired and ready to be collected, whenever you want.'

'I'm on my way.'

'Whenever you want,' he repeats. 'There's no rush.'

There is a rush. I'm in a hurry to live my life.

I stand outside my house waiting for the taxi. The video has finally gone. The prostitute came exactly on time and picked it up. No words. No nothing. I've got the camera with me and I will post it from Scotland. I can't really face explaining. I notice that Oliver's car is gone. A large 'For Sale' sign is nailed to the fence of his house. I would've liked to say goodbye to him.

As the taxi arrives, I open the letterbox and collect the letters which have accumulated in the past few days. My eyes light up when I see Sophie's wedding invitation. I'm so happy for her. Among the letters there's an old piece of paper ripped from a notebook. It has several scribbles and some stains in one corner.

My blood freezes.

It's Amy's handwriting.

Dear Megan,

You've always thought my life was perfect, but it's not. Your husband has given me unconditional support and I'm about to run away from Oliver's physical and mental abuse. It was too risky to tell you until Jamie and I were safe. I'm sorry you felt cheated on. There was no such deception.

I hope you get better and leave hospital soon.

The paper smells like cigarettes. Amy didn't smoke, but Oliver does. This is a letter she wrote to me before she died on that Wednesday I was hospitalised. The day after she should have left Oliver. Now we both know the truth. Will it do Oliver any good to know the truth?

I make a paper ball and throw it away.

'Good morning,' says the young shop assistant at the dry cleaner's. 'Here you are. The coat is clean and the lining is fixed. It's as good as new.'

I look at the coat through the plastic and remember Mum wearing it as she held my hand on the way to school. This coat is like a talisman that protects me and brings me luck.

'Thank you.'

'One moment. This was also left inside.' He puts a small bag on the counter with an object in it.

'What is that?'

'An inhaler, I think.'

'An inhaler?'

My heart accelerates.

'Yeah.'

I stare at the inhaler, but I'm not afraid any more.

'It's not mine,' I reply emphatically.

'It was in the pocket. You must've left it there. You don't know how many things people leave in their pockets by accident.'

'By accident?'

'Yes, by accident.' The shop assistant hesitates.

The seconds pass slowly, and a slight stinging comes over my cheeks. Sometimes you go out looking for the truth without realising that the truth is closer than you think.

'It was not an accident. It was revenge for a betrayal.'

The shop assistant's eyes and mouth open wide, but no words come out.

'You can throw it away,' I say with determination.

I straighten my back and leave the shop with my head up. The clouds have given way to a cold and clear light. The sun is shining like a happy child. I take a deep breath and step to the right.

My uncle carried many sins to be forgiven, but he had one sin that he was not to blame for: he was born without a heart. At least he spent his life believing that he did have one, so I wonder if I can forgive him. He did some good things, after all.

I take my phone from my bag and make a call. After five rings, a baritone voice answers.

'Megan? Is that you?'

'Tom, I need to see you. We need to talk.'

ACKNOWLEDGMENTS

To you, my readers, for letting me tell you this story.